Advance Praise for
AfterMath

"This book is a gift to the culture."

—Amy Schumer, writer, actor, and activist

"Lucy's story of grief and healing packs an emotional punch that will tug at your heartstrings long after you've read the last page."

—Edith Cohn, author of *Birdie's Billions*

"*AfterMath* is gorgeously written, infinitely heart-wrenching, and tragically timely. Lucy's voice is powerful and distinct. I loved this novel."

—Leslie Margolis, author of *Ghosted*, *We Are Party People*, and the Maggie Brooklyn Mysteries

"*AfterMath* is both heartbreaking and filled with hope. Gentle, nuanced, and honest, Isler's extraordinary debut will stay with readers long beyond the final page."

—Alex Richards, author of *Accidental*

"Parents aren't perfect, friendships aren't perfect, and life most certainly isn't perfect, but this novel comes pretty close to perfect in its fearless and compassionate exploration of the sorrows, struggles, and hard-won maturing of a spunky twelve-year-old as she deals with the aftermath of loss. The losses are real, the pain is real, but so—the author persuades us—is the saving grace of loving connection."

—Judith Viorst, author of *The Tenth Good Thing about Barney*

"Emily Barth Isler handles so many potentially explosive topics with grace and subtlety but also with enormous assurance and power. This is a brave, important and even essential novel."

—Yona Zeldis McDonough, author of *The Bicycle Spy* and *Courageous*

AFTERMATH

Emily Barth Isler

🕊 CAROLRHODA BOOKS
MINNEAPOLIS

Carolrhoda Books®
An imprint of Lerner Publishing Group, Inc.
241 First Avenue North
Minneapolis, MN 55401 USA

For reading levels and more information, look up this title at www.lernerbooks.com.

Cover illustration by Dien Ton That.

Main body text set in Bembo Std.
Typeface provided by Monotype Typography.

Library of Congress Cataloging-in-Publication Data

Names: Isler, Emily Barth, author.
Title: AfterMath / Emily Barth Isler.
Description: Minneapolis : Carolrhoda Books, [2021] | Audience: Ages 11–14. | Audience: Grades 4–6. | Summary: After her younger brother's death from a heart defect, twelve-year-old Lucy moves to a town that was devastated by a school shooting four years earlier, where she must navigate different kinds of grief.
Identifiers: LCCN 2020012553 (print) | LCCN 2020012554 (ebook) | ISBN 9781541599116 (trade hardcover) | ISBN 9781728417400 (ebook)
Subjects: CYAC: Grief—Fiction. | School shootings—Fiction. | Middle schools—Fiction. | Schools—Fiction. | Moving, Household—Fiction.
Classification: LCC PZ7.1.I874 Aft 2021 (print) | LCC PZ7.1.I874 (ebook) | DDC [Fic]—dc23

LC record available at https://lccn.loc.gov/2020012553
LC ebook record available at https://lccn.loc.gov/2020012554

Manufactured in the United States of America
1-48107-48760-4/8/2021

For Jim.
And for kids everywhere, who deserve
to go to school without fear.

PROLOGUE

I've never been a "pink" girl. I don't do princesses, ponies, or purple either, for that matter. Nothing against things that start with the letter *P*—I'm cool with penguins, prime numbers, peanut butter, and polynomials. I've just never liked pink.

"Choose one, Lucy. It's just wallpaper."

My mother is holding up three samples for me to see. One is pink, one is purple, and one, literally, has pink and purple ponies on it. What are the odds?

"You're wrinkling your nose," she says. She looks more sad than frustrated now, and I feel guilty.

"I'm twelve, Mom. Those are all kind of baby-ish." I try to *ex*plain, not *com*plain, like they teach you in therapy, but it's hard not to whine when your mom doesn't get you at all. And sometimes I don't feel like being extra nice even though Theo died.

He was my brother, but no one is cutting me any slack. Eight months on and I'm supposed to just embrace this "fresh start." As if a new school and a new town aren't enough, apparently there also has to be new wallpaper.

"Oh." My mother looks around the store, at the piles and piles of wallpaper samples and books full of them. I grab one and flip it open to a random page. It's floral but yellow, which is better.

"How about this?" I ask.

Now she's the one wrinkling her nose. "Yellow?"

I shrug. "I'm not committed to yellow. I can do green." My mom squints. "Or blue?" I say hesitantly.

My mother looks exasperated. "It seems like you don't even really care, Lucy."

"I don't," I say before I can stop myself. "I mean, I don't have strong feelings." I'm digging my toe into the industrial carpeting, as if, in the time it will take us to select wallpaper, I might be able to burrow into the ground and disappear.

"Well, I wish you did have strong feelings. It's your room. I want it to feel like home."

That's the problem. She wants it to be my room. She wants our new house to feel like home to me. But that's going to take a lot more than wallpaper.

We eventually settle on a fresh coat of paint. Blue, which is somehow not a controversial color for either of us.

It doesn't really matter. Blue paint isn't going to cover the fact that my room used to belong to a dead girl.

CHAPTER 1

Kenton, Maryland, and Queensland, Virginia, are 31.5 miles apart via the Baltimore-Washington Parkway, and the speed limit averages 45 mph along the way. However, via I-95, the towns are 38 miles apart but with a speed limit that averages 60 mph. Which is the faster route from Kenton to Queensland?

distance divided by speed = time
via the BW Parkway: 31.5 / 45 = 0.7 hours, or 42 minutes
via I-95: 38 / 60 = 0.63 hours, or about 38 minutes

But in reality, it might as well take seven million hours either way, because it seems like we're never going back there.

I live in a dead girl's house. I sleep in her room.

We knew this before we bought the house. Our real estate agent, Cheryl Ann (her full name—who on earth has the last name Ann???), mentioned it during our tour. Well, technically she only said that the couple who were selling the house had lost a daughter in the Queensland school shooting. But I know that my room is the one that used to belong to the daughter, because in my new closet, on the edge of the sliding doors—covered in an anemic, barely-there coat of white paint—I found a vertical set of hash marks, with a date written next to each mark and the name *Bette* written at the top.

It's a height chart. I had one just like it on my wall at home. My dad used to measure Theo and me every few months and draw lines where we stood to show how much we'd grown. Then he'd write our names and the date.

I often wonder who sleeps in my old room. Or in Theo's. Does the kid who lives there now know that they're sleeping in the room of a dead kid too?

Cheryl Ann also informed us that basically no one has moved to this town in the four years since the shooting, until my family. I don't blame everyone else for staying away. If it were up to me, I would have.

I hate that we moved. Especially to this town, where practically everyone lost someone. (In case you were wondering, Cheryl Ann lost a nephew.) My parents considered several empty houses here, because so many people have moved away over the past few years. The elementary school where the shooting took place was demolished afterward, and now there's a garden where it used to be. And the new elementary school across town is tall and modern, with prison-style lockdown safety features and bulletproof windows. The middle school, where I'll start seventh grade this fall, has gotten security upgrades too. Cheryl Ann made sure to tell us that.

We've driven by the memorial park a few times. Sadness seems to hang from the trees like brown, shriveled leaves that never fall off and never get replaced by fresh green ones. It feels like there's no rebirth here. Only death, and memories, and sadness.

"At least it's not our sadness or our memories," my dad said when I asked why we were moving to a town where so many people had died.

"And we got a heck of a deal on the house," my mom added. Which is kind of sick, when you think about it.

What my parents really care about is that we're not back in Kenton, where my brother died, where the family we used to be is buried with him.

Not much is changing for them. Both my parents work in Washington, DC, in government jobs. In Kenton, we were twenty-five miles outside DC, in a Maryland suburb with good schools and nice trees and pretty houses.

Now we're still twenty-five miles outside DC, just in the opposite direction, but it feels like a world away. Queensland, Virginia, is also a nice suburb with trees and houses. And you can buy the houses for cheap because no one else wants to.

"We won't stand out here," my parents say to each other when they think I'm not listening. But I'm always listening. I was almost seven when Theo was born. After he was diagnosed with his rare heart condition, I learned early on how to hear what Mom and Dad were muttering, even when I wasn't supposed to.

My parents get to keep their jobs. Their coworkers and schedules are the same. But for me, everything is new, and everything has changed.

For them, this place is an escape from the memories of the doctors and the specialists and the nightmare. For me, starting seventh grade in this place *is* the nightmare.

∞

"Lucy, what are you wearing to school tomorrow? Do you need help choosing something?"

I swallow my mashed potatoes. "Nope."

"That's not an answer, Lucy," my dad says.

"Yes it is," my mom pipes up, passing him the green beans. "I asked if she needs help."

Dad takes some beans with his fingers. "But you also asked what she's going to wear. And that isn't a yes-or-no question."

"Technically," I say quietly, "I said 'nope.' Not 'yes' or 'no.'"

No one hears me. Or rather, no one listens.

"She says she's got it under control," my mom says, her smile tense and tight. "We have to let her make some decisions."

"Okay, but I was just trying to increase communication. That is the point of these family dinners." If my dad realizes how ridiculous it is that he's talking about communication and ignoring me at the same time, he doesn't let on.

"Lucy," Mom says, almost looking at me but not quite, "I'll drive you there tomorrow. I can't come into the school, because I can't be late for work, but you won't have to take the bus on your first day. Okay?"

She always ends with "Okay?" but it's not actually a question. Or the question is always "Okay, did you hear me?" Not "Is that okay with you?"

I smile. I nod. Dinner's over.

It's my job to clear the table. After I load the dishes in the dishwasher—stacking them all facing the same way, just how my mother likes them—I linger by the kitchen sink and watch my parents. They sit at our brand-new dining room table, in chairs that are stiff and way too formal-looking. The chairs are upholstered in velvet: hard to get comfortable on and impossible to clean. My mom fell in love with this house mostly because of the dining room, something we didn't have in our old house. Here, she wants everything to be different. Everything is definitely different, that's for sure. But, like an unbalanced equation, "different" doesn't equal "better."

I'm behind the half-partition wall, so they can't see me, but I can see and hear everything. So I study them.

My parents are triangles. They are all sharp edges and straight lines, corners and angles. They are pointy and firm. Since Theo died, I've noticed how hard it is to hug a triangle. Where do you put your arms? Where do you rest your head?

Together they form a square, but I don't fit in it. There's no room.

I am a line. Theo was a line. We both extended, until his line stopped. Mine continues, but I don't know how to make it pierce through the triangles of my parents sitting at the dinner table, accidentally brushing arms in the hall. I don't know how to make an angle and then another, to turn back around and get back to where they are. I am a line, and I just keep going. Alone.

I used to get so desperately sad thinking of Theo being all alone in death. I particularly worried about him dying in his sleep, without anyone noticing for a while. So I started regularly sneaking into his room after he fell asleep for naps or even in the middle of the night. I'd put one of my favorite stuffed animals in his crib with him. Then I'd creep back to my own room, satisfied that at least he had Cuddles or Tiger for company, in case that was the day he would start his long journey alone to whatever was after life.

Queensland Middle School's main office has vibrant 1970s carpet and pea-green walls. It's easy enough to find when I walk in the front entrance, thanks to a big sign above it with four arrows pointing to the left. Inside, it's less clear where I am supposed to go.

I stand for a while between what seem like two different reception desks, feeling lost, until a woman who looks like she's worked there since before the 1970s carpet was laid out pops up from out of nowhere and waves me over to the desk on the right.

"You're Lucy Rothman," she says flatly.

I look around, as if maybe there's a sign above me with my name and four arrows pointing down. "How did you know?" I ask, not wanting to sound rude, but genuinely surprised that she knows who I am. And that she didn't ask, she just pronounced.

The lady shrugs. "Haven't had a new student start here in a long time." And she hands me a stack of papers. Her voice never wavers from a bored monotone, and her eyeglasses slip lower and lower down the bridge of her nose as she stares at me, though that does not seem to bother her.

"Welcome to Queensland Middle School. We hope you enjoy seventh grade." She says this with such robotic, expressionless boredom that I almost laugh. Maybe I'm just nervous.

I'm so distracted by the receptionist that I don't notice the other person in the office until the woman gestures to her. "Mara is going to lead you around school until you get the lay of the land."

I turn to look. Mara is tall and pretty, with long blond hair and a large, funny-shaped freckle on her right cheek that doesn't at all make her less beautiful. If she thinks the robotic receptionist is funny too, she doesn't let on.

"It's nice to meet you," she says to me.

I smile and mumble, "You too," and follow Mara outside the glass enclosure of the office. "I have art first with—" I start to say, but she cuts me off.

"I was in one of the classrooms where kids hid in the closet," she tells me. For a moment I have absolutely no idea what she means. Until it hits me all at once, like a bomb dropping in the middle of the hallway right at my feet, creating a hole in the ground that only I can see. *BOOM.*

Mara doesn't seem aware that it's a bomb. But to me, it feels like I've just stepped off a cliff into that crater and can't find the parachute cord to pull, let alone figure out what to say to this.

I know all about the town. Anyone who has ever watched the news in America has heard of Queensland, where a gunman broke into the elementary school and went on a shooting spree. I just assumed that, the way I don't plan to mention Theo to anyone here, no one would be talking about the shooting. To me, it seems like Coping 101. Don't talk about your tragedy in public.

Instead, it's all Mara is talking about.

"Our teacher was shot, of course. I heard the gunshots, but I didn't see anyone die," she tells me as we walk to art class together. "At least not that I remember. I have PTSD, and I blocked a lot of it out. My therapist says I might remember more someday, but my dad says it's better if I don't."

I nod, my head ringing. It all sounds completely surreal. I don't know what to say. Honestly, I'm thinking about Mara's plaid dress, and how, compared to it, my jeans and ironic Pac-Man shirt look stupid. And I immediately feel terrible for thinking about clothing when Mara is talking about death and tragedy. It's just not what I expected.

"Well, now that's out of the way," she says.

Maybe Mara thinks I wanted to know where she was during the shooting, like I would have asked if she hadn't offered first. Maybe other people she's met have been curious, and rude enough to ask, because that's all outsiders know about Queensland.

And now, like it's all so very normal, she announces, "This is art." We've reached a room at the end of the hall. The school is shaped like an octagon, and all eight sides/hallways look identical to me. Normally, I would chart the octagon out in my mind, bisect it, cut it into triangles, and arrange it in my mind till it made geometric sense. But I'm still distracted by the details of the shooting that I've gotten from Mara, and I can't quite map it. I am never going to learn my way around.

"Thanks," I say weakly. I shift my backpack from one shoulder to the other, noticing that Mara just carries a few books in a tote bag.

A boy walks by us—shorter than Mara, with curly, red hair. He nods to Mara and disappears into the art room.

"That's Donny. His twin brother died in the shooting. They were identical twins. Isn't that weird? Like, his parents have this exact replica to watch grow up, but they're still sad. You know?" *Boom* goes another bomb.

"I'll be back at the end of the period to help you to your next class," Mara says, flicking a strand of corn silk hair out of her eyes.

The fluorescent lights quiver above us. A bell chimes over the loudspeaker. I want to tell Mara not to bother coming back, but I know I would never find my way in this horrible octagon, so I just wave and mutter "Thanks" as I head into the art room.

Donny is there, in a sea of other kids who—it hits me fully now—are all survivors. They would've been in third grade when the shooting happened at their elementary school. All the kids who died were third graders. Of course I knew this intellectually already, but between the barrage of unexpected details and the face-to-face reality of the humans behind the news coverage, it's jarring. They've all known each other forever, gone through tragedy together. They all lost friends or are permanently affected by the events— I don't need to hear each one's individual story to know that. The statistics speak for themselves.

My personal statistics aren't as straightforward. It's very unlikely that anyone else would ever walk into the situation I'm in. There's a .000000001 percent chance that another elementary school would have another massacre like this one *and* that, four years later, another girl like me would join the class that suffered the heaviest losses.

My entire situation is highly unlikely, when you look at the numbers. Improbable. So was Theo's. Chances of him being born with his particular heart condition are one in ten million. How do you like those odds? Chances of him dying, though, once he got to be over two years old without any improvement, were very "good," not that anything about dying is good. But, statistically speaking, those were good odds. Lucky us.

∞

Art is pretty self-explanatory, a good first class to have. Most of the period is taken up with typical first-day filler: the teacher trying to match names with faces, explaining what unit we'll start the year with, having us do a simple intro exercise. It all feels incredibly normal, which is a huge relief.

I can tell that my classmates are watching me, though. While we're working on the mini art assignment that the teacher has given us, the girl in front of me turns around and asks where I'm from. "Maryland," I say.

"You're the first new kid we've had in a long time," she says matter-of-factly, just like the receptionist. "Because of the shooting."

She proceeds to tell me that she survived the shooting because she was standing behind a teacher, who was killed instead. And before I can respond, she turns back around and resumes drawing on her worksheet.

The normality of the morning is shattered. Is every single introduction at this school going to involve the shooting's gory details? This girl didn't even tell me her name. I think it's Heather, if I'm remembering the roll call right. Or is Heather the girl next to her? I do my best to focus on this instead of on what she said.

I don't know how, but Mara manages to arrive at the doorway just after the bell rings to signal that first period is over. Next she leads me to Spanish, where I'm seated next to a girl named Rosemary who's wearing an owl-shaped pin on her shirt.

"I like your pin," I tell her. Maybe conversations will go better if I'm the one to start them.

"I wear it for my best friend, Jessica," she says. "She loved owls. I was holding her hand when she was shot."

My emotions split in two directions. One is horror for this poor girl, like being punched in the chest and the gut all at once. But the other thing I feel is anger—at my parents. No one prepared me for this. Shouldn't my parents have anticipated it? Didn't they think about what it would be like for me to be surrounded by survivors who've been forever marked by the tragedy—where the names of ghosts come before those of the living?

"I'm so sorry," I say. Because even though I know how empty that phrase can feel, having been on the receiving end of it, what else can I say?

Rosemary shrugs. "She lives on in our memories." I wonder who told her to say that—her therapist? Her minister? Her parents?

Our rabbi, Rabbi Steve, back home in Kenton, always said that to me about Theo. "Don't be afraid to talk about your brother. He will live on in your memories."

I wonder if Rabbi Steve gave that same advice to my parents. If so, they're doing a crappy job. Maybe I am too, because it's my plan to keep Theo a secret at my new school. His death and the deaths from the shooting here are completely different. The two can't exist in the same formula. How can I ever tell these kids about Theo without feeling like I'm some-how minimizing their experience or simplifying their pain? I'm in an impossible situation.

I can't help noticing that Rosemary is wearing a dress, like Mara and Heather from art and most of the other girls I've seen. I make a mental note to wear a dress tomorrow. And get a tote bag.

∞

At lunchtime, Mara walks me to the cafeteria and gives me the lay of the land: "That table on the far end is the band kids." Most of whom seem to be ignoring each other in favor of texting. "The one next to it is mainly people on cross-country, but a few soccer players." I nod, because those kids look like the jocks at my old school. That's something I can relate to, at least.

"Over there"—Mara points in the opposite direction—"is the activists' table. Their parents are all involved in gun laws and stuff, ever since the shooting. They do a bunch of marches and lobby days in DC." I spot Donny, the redhead from earlier. Otherwise, to me these kids look almost identical to the first group—on their phones, texting away or

Googling something or whatever people do. I don't know, because I don't have a smartphone. I put it on my mental list, below dresses and a tote bag, but I know my parents won't say yes.

She gestures to another table: "Those are the artsy kids." I wonder if I should be writing it all down and where I'm supposed to fit in.

"I don't actually have this lunch period," Mara says, looking at the clock, "so I have to go."

She starts to leave, but I call after her. "Wait! Where do I sit?" People stream past us carrying trays of pizza and fries.

Mara shrugs. "Anywhere," she says, though that's obviously not at all true. I know from my old school that it's really important who sits where at lunch.

It wasn't exactly simple for me there, either. In the long years while Theo was sick, a lot of kids wouldn't come near me, as if maybe heart conditions were contagious. None of them knew what to say to me. Molly was always there for me, but more than once I caught her looking over at the popular kids' table with longing, as if I—not her love of puppets and *Sesame Street*—were the only thing keeping her from being with them.

When I told Molly we were moving, I swear I

saw a hint of relief in her eyes mixed in with sadness. Things with the other kids at school hadn't gotten better after Theo died. They avoided me. Maybe they felt that grief, or death itself, could spread to them by mere association. I had spent so many years never inviting anyone over to my house, not having birthday parties, because Theo's health was so unpredictable, that it seemed too late to start making other friends. Their groups, their intricate alliances, were already firmly in place.

So I know that you can't just walk up to any old lunch table and take a seat. I consider what Mara identified as the "activists' table." I quickly discard that idea, though, because it would mean justifying why I feel like I belong. Explaining that my parents used to be into fundraising for research to benefit kids with Theo's kind of heart defect would mean disclosing that I had a brother who died, and that's literally the last thing in the world I want to tell these kids.

All of this is moot, anyway, because most of the tables in my new cafeteria don't have a single free chair.

I spot one table that's empty except for one girl. I figure I might be able to sit there, as far from her as possible. That's easy to calculate because the table is a circle, so I just choose the chair at the other end of the imaginary diameter. I've brought a book, and all I want is to read it in peace.

The girl barely acknowledges me. Her eyes kind of flick over me, but she quickly goes back to whatever she's scribbling in a notebook. I brace myself to listen to her story about the shooting.

But the girl at the table doesn't volunteer anything. The squeezing of my chest eases somewhat. She doesn't seem bothered by my presence. Her hair is dyed black, and she's wearing a lot of makeup. The mascara on her eyelashes is so thick I can see little clumps from across the table. Like all the other girls, she's wearing a dress, but it's not any kind or style I've ever seen a kid wear. It's what my mom would call "vintage"—clearly from another era. The girl also wears fancy gladiator-style sandals, which is a little strange, but I don't spend any more time sizing her up. I have my book to read and a sandwich to eat.

And the rest of this day to get through.

CHAPTER 2

A square is a regular quadrilateral, which means that it has four equal sides and four equal angles. What happens when one side is gone? Is it still a square?

No.

If a family has four members, and one is gone, are we still a family?

"Did you make tons of friends?" my mom asks at dinner.

"Uh-huh," I say, my mouth full of salad. Mom only ever asks questions at dinner when my mouth is too full to say much.

I did not, in fact, make tons of friends. I did not make any. But there's no need to tell my mom that.

I don't know how to explain to her that death hung over my day like a thick quilt. That hardly anyone talked to me and that the people who did brought up the shooting casually, like it's always on their minds—or maybe they just think it's on mine?

"What books are you going to read in English this year?" asks Dad. He's barely touched the food on his plate. He must've had a bad day.

"I don't know yet," I tell him. My dad got his masters in literature before taking a civilian job at the Pentagon. He always wants to know what books I'm reading. He never asks what we're doing in math, even though that's my favorite subject.

"Didn't you get a syllabus?" he pushes on.

I put down my water glass. "I don't know what that means," I say.

"A syllabus is a list of reading materials and lessons and topics for a class," he says impatiently, as if I should know.

"She's in seventh grade, Beau," my mom says.

Dad drops his silverware with a clatter. "So? It's a good word to know."

∞

I have an email from Molly—a response to the one I sent her right after school today.

I can't believe your parents didn't give you an iPhone. It's the least they could have done, after they dragged you away. This sucks. I miss you. School sucks this year without you. Everything sucks. But I'm glad you're finally starting school. We've already been in session for two weeks. I'm sure you'll make friends soon.

I click *reply*, but I realize I have nothing to say. I've already told Molly that I haven't found any friends and my parents are being themselves and our house used to belong to a dead girl's family. I told her that the girls wear dresses and carry tote bags and that everyone but me has a smartphone. I can't think of a single thing to add.

So I shut down the computer and get into bed. I haven't brushed my teeth or washed my face, but I'm too tired to care. I lie there looking at the ceiling, wondering if the dead girl who used to have this room had a smartphone when she was alive. I know she was only eight, but some kids get phones when they're really young. Especially in Queensland, it seems, but I don't know if that was the case before the shooting. I bet a lot changed.

Even though I'm exhausted, I can't fall asleep. Too many thoughts run through my head. Some are math thoughts, which I like—the 12s table is one of my favorites to go through when I'm nervous or anxious—but there are other thoughts that don't have concrete answers, and those kinds of thoughts, I don't like.

So I get up, not sure where I'm going, and that's when it catches my eye. A small piece of paper, on the floor of my room. Near the corner. I pick it up. It's typed and printed out.

A teacher asks a student, "What is 2n + 2n?"
The student answers, "I don't know. It's 4n to me!"

I laugh in spite of myself. But I also look around. Where did it come from? Is it possible it was here the whole time?

Could it have belonged to the girl who used to live here? Did she like math too?

No. That is ridiculous, I tell myself. There's no way this math joke is left over from when Bette was alive. There is no way this scrap of paper survived the cleaning crew and the people who painted my walls blue and the two sets of movers and real estate agents in between. Or my mom on her scrub-the-rooms-like-your-life-depends-on-it quest, for that matter.

There is no way.

And yet.

I get into bed, and I can finally fall asleep. Because there is a tiny part of me that wants to believe the joke is hers. Somehow that makes me feel less alone.

∞

"You live in Bette's old house," a boy says to me at the bus stop the next morning.

I nod, shoving my hands into the pockets of my dress. I didn't have time to get a tote bag, and the smartphone request was rejected as I thought it would be, but I did manage to wear a dress.

"That wasn't a question," the boy says, taking a step toward me. "I was telling you."

"Oh," I say. It feels like that's all I ever say. And I stop myself before asking if she liked math or jokes, even though I want to know.

"We were friends," he tells me. "Our parents were close."

"I'm sorry for your loss," I say. People said that to me all the time right after Theo died.

A few more kids walk up to the bus stop. I notice none of the girls are wearing dresses, even though they all were the day before, and I scowl, frustrated. Is there some kind of dress code text that goes out daily, stating that everyone has to wear a dress on the first day but can wear jeans the second?

Another boy approaches us, taller and bigger than Bette's friend. This one has blond hair and clear blue eyes. "Are you the one who was sitting with Avery at lunch yesterday?" he asks me.

I look back and forth between the two boys. There are several other kids at the bus stop now, and it seems like they're all watching us. I've never felt more like a solitary number.

"Of course it was her," snaps Bette's friend. "How many new girls do you think there are in town?"

"Just the one," says the big blond boy. The sun dances through the trees behind us.

"Who is Avery?" I ask. I wish the bus would arrive already.

"Dark hair, lots of makeup." The girl who answers looks familiar—I'm pretty sure she's in a few of my classes. Elisa, I think.

"You don't want to hang out with Avery," says the first boy, Bette's friend. He's too close to me, and I can feel my hands sweating.

"Give her space, Dave," says the big blond boy, and I'm grateful. They all take a step back, and behind them, I see with relief that the bus is pulling up.

"Sorry," says Dave.

I follow them all onto the bus, where I mercifully find a seat alone. I'd rather be alone than sit with any of them. But I realize I never got to ask why I shouldn't hang out with Avery.

∞

I do hang out with her, though. Or, at least, I sit with Avery again at lunch. She's the closest thing I can find to sitting by myself. I just want to read my *Coding for Kids* book, and she leaves me alone. I almost ask Avery what her story is, why the kids were warning me about her, but I am nowhere near that bold.

Avery doesn't give me a chance, anyway. She never once looks up from her notebook. I stare at her for a while, once I'm sure she's not going to try to talk to me. It's hard to tell what she really looks like underneath so much eye makeup, and I wonder what color her obviously dyed hair used to be. In spite of myself, I wonder where she was on the day of the shooting.

I remember where I was when I heard about it. I was eight, the same age as the kids who died.

Theo was in the hospital, which is how I was watching the news. I watched a lot of news in various waiting rooms. Between his heart issues and his weak immune system, he was in the hospital more than he was at home. So I was too.

I can practically see that newscast in my mind. The very pretty Asian American woman with really shiny hair was talking about the stock market when she paused, listened to something being said in the tiny speaker in her ear, and said something like, "We have a breaking story. We will be bringing you live details as they come in. An elementary school in Virginia is on lockdown . . ."

The news covered the shooting wall-to-wall for days, and since my parents were taking turns by Theo's side, I watched a lot of coverage. Had they realized what I was seeing, my parents would've made the nurses change the channel or something, but I don't think they even registered that the shooting had happened until days later. They were so focused on what was going on with Theo that they had no sense of what day it was, let alone what was unfolding on TV.

I remember how someone interviewed the shooter's dad on the news. He looked like a bunch of dads I know. He had a beard and wore a gray hoodie.

He cried a lot, and I felt sorry for him. He said he and his son had been estranged, and later I asked my dad what that meant.

"Why do you want to know?" he asked, taking off his glasses and rubbing the bridge of his nose like he does when he's really tired, or really stressed, or both.

I shrugged. We were waiting in the drive-through line at Roy Rogers, picking up chicken to bring back to Mom at the hospital, plus fries to try to coax Theo to eat. "I heard it somewhere."

Dad sighed distractedly, reaching for his wallet to pay the girl at the window. As we got closer, I recognized her as the daughter of one of my mom's friends, but I didn't say hi. I turned my face away as we approached and hoped she didn't recognize us. I wasn't in the mood for small talk.

"Estranged is when two people, usually family, aren't in touch anymore. Like they've lost contact, or one has decided to cut the other out of their life or something."

"Thanks," I said. So it was a simple subtraction equation—person minus another person equals estrangement. And I thought again of that crying man, the father of the shooter from that seemingly faraway school.

Now I wonder if he still lives in Queensland. The crying father, not the shooter, since everyone who ever watched the news knows the shooter didn't make it out of the school. He shot himself last.

It's for the best that the elementary school got torn down, I think. It's one thing for me to sleep in the dead girl's old room, or for these kids to sit around talking about their friends who were shot, but it's another to go to class in a building where it all took place.

I guess that's why my parents felt like they had to move. When they decided Theo should come home from the hospital to die in the living room, with all of us around him, I never imagined it meant we would have to leave someday. But being there just became too hard. How do you watch cartoons in the morning, sitting on the spot where your brother drowned in his own lungs?

∞

"How are you liking it?" Mara asks me as she guides me to my last class of the day.

I paste on a small, plastic smile. "It's fine," I say.

I have math for eighth period, and I'm looking forward to that. It isn't just my favorite subject; it's my thing. Some kids do ballet. Some are really good at music. I do math. I *love* math. I love how it's predictable and it makes sense. There is always one correct answer.

Mara nods. She flicks her hair around, which I am realizing must be her signature move, or a tic, because she does it all the time.

"I like your dress," she says. There's a hint of a twinkle in her eye, and I can't tell if she's being nice or somehow mean.

I blush. "I saw everyone wearing dresses yesterday . . ."

"That's a first-day-of-school thing, mostly," Mara says, as if that would have been obvious.

"Now I know that," I say. It's supposed to be 85 degrees tomorrow, but I will definitely be wearing jeans. I don't want to stick out at this school any more than I already do.

Nobody's said anything about the shooting today. Nobody's said anything to me at all, actually, except for Mara. I've overheard plenty of conversations about TV shows and games and whether the cafeteria will ever serve chocolate milk again, but none of them have been directed at me.

Before we get to my math classroom, Mara pulls

me aside, leaning against a rust-colored locker. "So I heard you're sitting with Avery at lunch." She looks at me with her big blue eyes, and again I wonder if she's being nice or mean. It's so hard to tell.

"Yeah. That's where there was an empty seat," I say. "You told me to sit anywhere." I realize how whiny and small I sound, and I feel like I might cry, though I don't know why.

Mara stands up straight. She's a full head taller than I am. "Just sit somewhere *else*, okay?" she says, tugging at her jeans and doing a hair flick.

"Why?" I ask, but Mara is already a few feet ahead, walking down the hall. She doesn't hear me, or if she does, she doesn't answer.

In math, there are unknowns and there are variables. Sometimes teachers use the terms interchangeably, but they're not quite the same. An unknown is a specific number that you have to solve for in an equation. A variable is a number that can change, depending on the rest of the formula it's in. It's hard to tell if I'm dealing with variables like what I'm supposed to wear or unknowns, like whatever makes it unacceptable to sit with Avery.

A voice behind me makes me jump. "Hi there, Lucy." It's Mr. Jackson, my math teacher.

I turn and shyly say hi back.

Mr. Jackson is my favorite person at school so far. He's younger than the other teachers, and he has a sense of humor, and he genuinely loves math—you can just tell.

"Today," he says as we all take our seats, "we will be discussing infinity."

He stands at his desk.

"I'm going to demonstrate the concept of infinity now. This is an example of something called Zeno's paradox, where you cut a distance in half, and then in half again, and so on. Are you all watching? Here goes." He turns his back to us, facing the wall. "I'm going to walk to the wall, okay?"

Everyone is looking at him. I feel myself smiling without even meaning to.

"I'm going to start by walking halfway there," he says, rolling up his light blue shirt sleeves as he talks.

"Okay," Mr. Jackson says as he takes a giant step forward, "Do you all agree I'm halfway to the wall?"

A few people say yes, but most of us just nod.

"And now I'll take a step that's halfway from where I am now to the wall." This step is slightly smaller. "And again, another step from where I am, halfway to the wall."

He keeps doing this, his steps getting smaller and smaller as he goes half the distance each time.

As Mr. Jackson gets so close to the wall that he's almost touching it, he turns to us. "So, do you see? I will never actually get to the wall. Because I'll always be taking a step that's half the distance from me to it."

He gazes around the room, his eyes making contact with each student, one by one. "Do you understand?"

Some people nod. I'm not smiling anymore. In fact, for the second time in five minutes, I feel like I might cry. I don't understand.

"But what about when you're touching the wall?" asks the boy in front of me.

"Good question, Joshua. That's one I'm going to have to put off, though, because it's really a physics question, a matter of—well—*matter*, and space. For now, though, do you see my point about infinity? How there are an infinite number of steps between me and the wall? Because any time there's a distance, there's always half the distance, and more to go."

More people nod, like everyone is getting it. I still don't.

"Lucy?" says Mr. Jackson. "Do you have a question?"

Everyone turns to me. I feel tears in my eyes. I wish I could make myself disappear.

I shake my head, and my classmates look away. Mr. Jackson is still watching me, though, looking over at me every few minutes through the rest of the class period.

This isn't right. Math is numbers. It's undeniable truths. It's things you can depend on. The infinity thing just doesn't make sense to me. No matter how hard I try, I cannot picture it in my head. I can't see the numbers.

When the bell finally rings, I'm exhausted from trying to hold myself together. I just want to go home and cry, even though I'm not sure exactly why. Something about infinity, about never actually getting anywhere, never reaching your destination, makes me feel incredibly sad.

∞

On the way home, the bus isn't nearly as crowded as it is in the morning. A lot of kids stay after school for activities. I've never been much of an after-school activity kid. It was too hard with Theo.

I take a seat by myself about halfway back and notice Joshua, the boy from my math class, in the seat across the aisle from me. He's reading a comic book, but I can't see what it is. What I can see, though, is how his dark, curly hair flops over his forehead and his thick eyelashes flick up and down as his eyes go from page to page. He catches me looking at him, and for a second, I smile. I want to ask what comic book he's reading. I want to ask him to explain the infinity thing to me, but I don't say anything to him.

A few more kids get on the bus, and soon it pulls away, toward the house I'm supposed to now call home.

∞

My parents are still at work, so I use my key to let myself inside. There is yet another new rug in our house that I almost trip over. This one's on the floor of the dining room. My mom is so determined to "make our house a home" that she adds something to it almost every day. It's like all the energy she used to spend on taking care of Theo is now going into this new place where we're supposed to be starting over.

I head straight to the computer in my dad's study. I don't even stop to wash my hands, even though I know I'm supposed to every time I come in the house. It's an old rule, back from when Theo was alive, but now that he's not here to get sick(er) from my germs, I don't see the point.

The subject of Molly's email is *DRAMA!!!!* I can practically hear her voice in my mind as I read it to myself.

I joined the drama club today!!!!! OMG so excited. Of course, I wish you were here to join it with me, but I'm still pretty excited. Does your new school have a drama club? If so, are you going to join?

I've been hanging out with Sophie Lamar, and she's cool, but I miss you!

I don't know if it's the email itself, or just the whole day's worth of holding it in, but I burst into tears. I wanted to join the drama club. I wanted to do that with Molly. I think Sophie Lamar is mean and bossy, and I hate that she's Molly's new friend. I hate that I've been replaced.

My being a math nerd always worked out pretty well for my parents. Math games and problem sets are the kinds of extracurricular activities you can do easily in hospital waiting rooms, unlike soccer or ballet . . . or drama club. And my parents didn't have to feel guilty because I was doing something "academic" and "worthwhile" while they tended to Theo. Better than just watching TV all the time, even though I did a lot of that too.

But this year, I was going to actually do something. I was going to join the drama club with Molly.

By the time my parents get home, I'm feeling better. Or at least I'm feeling more like I can pretend that I am.

At dinner, Dad asks right away, "Second day of school was better, right?"

I smile and nod, because how do you say no to that? My dad has a way of asking questions so that you can't really give any answer besides the one he wants to hear. "You slept well last night?" is a favorite. What am I supposed to say—"Actually, no, I didn't"? Or sometimes he'll ask, "Aren't you so happy right now?" like when we see a beautiful sunset or have a nice meal. Again, I can't really reply, "Actually, no, I'm kind of miserable."

It started when Theo got really sick. Dad would say things to Mom like, "He'll get better, won't he?" And she would say, "Of course!" Or he'd ask,

"Doesn't it seem like Theo is stronger today?" And the only kind reply is "Yes!"

But Theo didn't get better, and he wasn't stronger. His heart got weaker and weaker, and he kept getting infections, until his body basically shut down. We knew it would. There was the chance it could have been another six or eight years, at the most, but based on the statistics for his rare condition, we always knew that he wouldn't live past the age of thirteen.

Now that I'm so close to that age, thinking about it feels weird. I know Theo is gone anyway, and nothing is going to change that, but getting older than his greatest life expectancy feels like another way I'm unintentionally dishonoring his memory, surpassing him. Doing something he was never, ever going to be able to do.

CHAPTER 3

Queensland had a population of 2,500 people. Of these, 32 people were killed in the shooting. Another 24 people were significantly wounded (physically). What percentage of people were killed or significantly injured? Solve for x.

$x/100 = (24+32)/2500$
$x/100 = 56/2500$
$x = 5600/2500$
$x = 2.24\%$

But in terms of what percentage were emotionally wounded . . . my guess is 100 percent.

At the end of my third day of school—a long, hot day spent wearing jeans despite the heat because I want to fit in—Mr. Jackson pulls me aside after math.

"Hey, Lucy. How's it going?"

I just smile and shrug, because I'm not sure if this is just a rhetorical "How's it going?" or a "How are you liking school?" or a "No, really, how are you feeeeeeling?" kind of question. Until I remember that no one at school knows about my dead brother. So I relax, certain it can't be that last one.

Mr. Jackson takes his glasses off and bends down a tiny bit so our eyes are almost on the same level.

"Lucy," he says, really looking at me like he cares, "I'm going to be teaching an after-school class I thought you might like."

My stomach drops. *He knows I didn't understand the infinity thing.* I'm mortified. Math is my best subject, and here I am, already failing it at this new school. I just stare at him.

But he continues like everything is okay. "It's a course in mime and nonverbal communication."

My face must be broadcasting how confused I am—is this related to math somehow? Is it supposed to sound fun? Mr. Jackson smiles, and I relax a little.

"Before I became a middle school math teacher, I studied theater in college," he says. "So I'm leading our theater extracurriculars this year. And the seventh-grade unit is mime."

"Oh, cool." I'm still not sure what this has to do with me or what I'm supposed to say.

"I thought maybe you'd like to take the class," he says, still hunched over to be closer to my height. "It's every Tuesday after school, starting next week, for the rest of the quarter."

"Oh," I say. Mime does not sound like fun to me. But I guess it could be *kind of* like drama.

"Will you think about it?" Mr. Jackson asks. He seems like he really wants me to. "I think it might be a nice chance to get to know some new friends."

He pats me on the shoulder and disappears down one of the octagon-sided hallways.

I'm still in a daze as I wait to get on the bus. I keep thinking of questions I wish I'd asked Mr. Jackson. *Am I in trouble? Is that why you think I need the mime class? Is it so obvious that I have no friends? Is this about me sitting with Avery at lunch? Or is this about the infinity concept, and the fact that I clearly don't get it?* I know he only asked me to think about it, but I feel like he thinks I really need this class, for some reason.

The bus pulls up, and I'm getting in line to file on when I hear a voice behind me.

"You dropped this."

It's Joshua, from my math class. He's smiling kindly and holding out a pencil. It takes me a second to realize it's mine.

"Oh. Thank you," I say at last. The kids behind us are getting impatient, but I can't stop looking at Joshua. It's a funny feeling, and I can't put a finger on it. I take the pencil, careful that our hands don't accidentally touch.

Once I'm sitting by myself in the middle of the bus, I see Joshua a few rows ahead. He can't see me, since he's facing forward, so I can stare as much as I want.

Earlier, in math class, I noticed this thing he did with his hands: he clenched his fists, alternating sides, the same number of times on each hand. Like he'd squeeze his left hand three times, and then his right hand three times. Sitting there in math, watching him do that, I had the sudden impulse to reach out and hold his hand. Not because I wanted to make him stop clenching his fists or anything, but just because I wanted to be holding his hand.

Now, on the bus, I blush just thinking about it. I've never held hands with a boy, besides Theo, and I don't think holding hands with your sick brother in a hospital bed counts.

All the way home, I look at Joshua a few rows ahead of me. I like the freckles on his right cheek, how they make a perfect isosceles triangle. I like that his hair sticks up every which way because of the curls. And I wish there were a way to ask if he's going to join Mr. Jackson's mime class after school.

∞

"Good third day, right?" Dad says at dinner.

"Yes," I say.

Mom piles salad on my plate. "Are the kids nice?"

I spear a leaf of lettuce and put it in my mouth. "I don't really know yet," I say.

"She needs to get to know some people," my dad says to my mom, as if I'm not there.

"Actually," I say, more loudly than usual, and they both look at me, surprised. "There's a class, after school. That I want to take. It's with my math teacher, Mr. Jackson."

My dad methodically cuts his chicken into tiny pieces, the knife scratching across the plate. "You want to take an after-school math class?"

"What do they do in an after-school math class, I wonder," my mom says to him.

"Maybe enrichment activities, or computer games."

"That doesn't sound very social," Mom mutters to her plate.

It's as if they've forgotten I'm there. "It's not a math class," I say. They both look at me.

"You said it was your math teacher," Dad says.

"She did," Mom agrees. "She definitely said it was her math teacher."

"Yes," I say patiently. "But it's a drama class. Mime, actually." I wait for a response.

My parents look at each other, puzzled.

"What does your math teacher know about mime?"

"Or drama?"

"Are you sure it's a mime class? Do people even do mime anymore these days?"

"I haven't heard of anyone doing mime."

I shrug. "He said something about nonverbal communication skills."

Mom looks at Dad. He raises his eyebrows, and she tilts her head.

"Could be interesting," she says.

"But how would she get home?" Dad wonders out loud.

"Yes, she'd miss the bus after school." Mom talks to him like I'm not there again.

"Maybe there's an activities bus?"

I clear my throat. "I could find out," I say quietly.

"Yes, find out," Dad says.

"Could be interesting," my mom says again. And they both finally look at me, but it's as if I'm a science experiment and they're evaluating how well I did or didn't work out.

CHAPTER 4

Every day, 7 American children and teens lose their lives because of gun violence.
Every day, 40 American children and teens are shot and survive.
Question: What is the total number of American children and teens shot every day?

Answer: 47

Before bed, I dash off an email to Molly.

It's really cool that you joined drama. I still hate it here. BUT I am taking a drama class too!!! It's a mime class, actually, but the teacher is sooooo amazing. He's this really incredible performer and he specifically asked me to join the class.

I have no idea if Mr. Jackson is an incredible performer, but he said he studied theater in college, and

I like watching him teach in math class, which is kind of like performing. It's not like Molly will ever know if anything I tell her is true or not. I could tell her that elephants roam the octagonal halls of my new school, acting as therapy pets for the traumatized students, and she'd have to take my word for it.

I'm only supposed to use the internet for email, math games, or school project research. My parents made this rule a long time ago, when Theo was sick and they didn't want me Googling his health issues. I think they didn't want me finding out that he was going to die, even though it was obvious. They talked about it right in front of me, as if I wasn't paying attention or couldn't understand. As if the words *terminal* or *demise* were so hard to figure out when the despair was written on my parents' faces. You couldn't have been in that house and not know. And it's not as if reading about it on the internet could have made me any sadder about it than I already was.

"With his life expectancy," my dad would say over the breakfast table, as if speaking in code, "we should be mindful of time."

I wanted to jump in and say, "Dad, I'm nine, not stupid," but I could see tears in his eyes, and in my mom's. I never told them I knew Theo was going to die; saying it out loud would have made it seem too real.

I survived that time by pretending it wasn't happening so that I didn't have to feel anything. The pain of lying was not nearly as bad as the crushing despair I would have summoned by bursting my parents' bubble of optimism. So when they sat me down to tell me, shortly after my tenth birthday, that things weren't looking good for Theo, I acted surprised.

"Oh no," I said. I tried to sound just as sad as I felt inside, but that was hard.

"It's okay to cry," my mom told me, squeezing my left arm. She was sitting on one side of me on the tiny love seat in the living room in our old house. My dad sat on my other side, already holding my right hand a little too tightly, as if keeping me safely connected to him.

So I do have some acting experience, after all.

"We're going to be okay," my dad told me. He and my mom looked at each other over my head, making an obtuse angle above an obtuse conversation. "We three are going to be okay."

But are we? We're not the same three people who made up a unit before Theo was born. Grief has turned us into fractions. Grief is made of shapes that don't fit together, equations that don't add up. And it follows us everywhere. It's in this house. My mother can redecorate and try to make it feel like home, she can replace all our furniture with new things that don't have our sad memories. But she can't replace Theo.

After I send my email to Molly, even though I'm not supposed to Google anything, I linger by the computer. There's a blank search bar on the screen. My parents are both downstairs, reading, and I know I'll hear them on the creaky steps coming up, so I'll have time to close the browser window and they'll never know.

I stare at the monitor. What do I want to ask the internet?

Avery, I think. Why everyone told me not to sit with her. But I have nothing to go on—I don't even know her last name. I search "Avery" and "Queensland, Virginia," but nothing interesting comes up.

I lean back in my dad's desk chair, taking in the photos on his desk. There's one of Mom and me from when I was two years old. We're on the beach, and she's holding both my hands, dunking me in the ocean. We look happy. We look normal, like death isn't part of our lives yet.

There's another picture on Dad's desk, one of Mom and Theo. It's from when he was a few months old, before he started to seem really sick. I wonder if that's how my dad wants to remember Theo. Because that would mean only a few months of Theo's life are worth remembering. Is that all there is, in Dad's mind?

Google's blank bar tempts me again, and I think of my room, on the other side of the wall from the office where I sit, the lone twin bed and the girl who slept in there before I did.

I search for "Queensland and Bette" and she pops right up. Elizabette Lane "Bette" Osceola, age eight, shot with five of her classmates and a teacher in the hallway outside their classroom. I shudder at the details. Like the specifics in my classmates' stories, they're hard to absorb. They make something that should be unimaginable feel horribly concrete.

There's a photo of Bette in one of the articles. She looks a lot like I did then. Tan skin, dark hair, ponytails. Average size, big smile. She's missing a front tooth in the picture, and I wonder if the new adult tooth had a chance to grow in before Bette was killed, or if she died missing that tooth. An incomplete equation.

I feel tears burning behind my eyes, and decide I've had enough. Maybe my parents aren't wrong to limit my time on the internet. I close the search window and shut down the browser. I dim the lights in the study the way my dad likes them and head back to my room, but once I'm sitting on the bed, all I can think of is Bette. Was her bed in this corner where mine is? It probably was, since the other walls have windows and this is the most logical place for a bed. Did she sit here, just as I am now, and imagine her future? She probably thought she'd live a long time. She probably imagined she'd at least live to get that front tooth. To Christmas or Hanukkah or some other holiday she loved. To college and marriage and babies, or whatever she wanted to do.

My dad peeks his head around my door. "Hey, pumpkin."

"Hey, Daddy."

He takes one step in and stops, hovering there in the doorway. "You good?"

I nod. "I'm good." I hope he can't see my hands grasping the comforter on my bed. If he doesn't, there's no way he'll guess that I'm trying not to cry as thoughts of Bette and my would-have-been class-mates crush my chest.

"Good night."

"Night, Dad."

I'm alone again when he closes the door, but I feel like I'll never really be alone in my room. Now that

I've opened the imaginary box of Bette's memory, she'll always be there with me. I picture her running her fingers over the smooth walls, hanging up posters of horses or puppies, lying on the floor staring at the ceiling as I often do. And somehow, instead of being sad or totally creeped out, I feel a little shiver of warmth run down my spine. As if there's a sense of connection between me and Bette. It's almost like having a friend.

I get the tiny piece of paper with the math joke from my desk drawer where I stashed it, and I try to think of something to add. Finally, I grab a pencil and write:

How do you make "seven" even?
You take away the "s" ☺

And I leave the paper there, on my desk, just in case some part of Bette—her soul, her ghost, her essence?—is going to look for it. I know that's ridiculous, but in spite of myself, I want it to be true.

∞

For months after Theo died, we'd find random toys and household items hidden in secret places. Theo would put small things in crevices we didn't even know existed. My mom says I did the same when I was his age, but I guess I was always there later to dig them out and keep playing.

At first, when we'd find Theo's hidden gems, it felt like any other time he'd been in the hospital for several nights. The house would seem so quiet without him, and then I'd be sorting through laundry and find his socks, and I'd remember that he was fighting for his life in the hospital and my parents weren't at work but at his bedside.

And once the hospice volunteers had come to clear out all the equipment that had created a makeshift hospital in our living room, I could pretend that Theo was just at the hospital again. I'd find his Superman underwear in the dryer, or the tiny Lego man he'd put in a drawer, or a silicone spatula that had been missing from the kitchen for months tucked under a couch cushion, and it still felt like life.

All through Saturday, I find myself thinking about those times, as I walk around our new house and wonder if Bette's parents had the same experiences. Did Bette's T-shirts in the dirty laundry hamper make them cry weeks after her death? Or did some helpful relative come in and rid the house of all reminders of her before those buried treasures could surprise them?

My mom turned Theo's bedroom into the guest room in our old house in less than a week. And then I'd hear her in there at night, crying, telling my dad she wished she hadn't cleared out all his stuff.

I wonder if my room—Bette's old room—was left untouched until we moved here, or if it was long ago changed over to a study or an exercise room.

Suddenly, it occurs to me that I don't know if Bette had siblings. I slide open my closet door to expose the edge with the height chart and peer through the light coat of paint. There seems to be only one set of marks, the one labeled *Bette*.

Now I picture her parents, alone and lost in their new home far away. I can't bear that idea, so I run back to the study and open the closet door there. I frantically search the doorframe and the back wall until I spot the faint notches. *Martin*, it says at the top, and I see marks going up to about three feet high, where they stop.

But instead of making me feel less sad for Bette's not-childless parents, I feel a new stab of sorrow. Martin, this little guy, shorter than Bette, must have been her younger brother. I stand next to the height chart and see that Martin's measurements stop around the same place on my body where Theo stood before he died. Meaning Martin and Theo were around the same size at some point.

Meaning somewhere, this family is missing a girl my age, and mine is missing a younger brother. We're like puzzles, missing different pieces, but we could never all fit together.

I sink down on the floor of the closet, between my dad's fancy, special occasion suits and my mom's raincoat, and let the tears come out.

∞

On Sunday, I wake to my mom climbing into my twin bed with me, trying to cuddle.

"Mom!" I whine. "What time is it?"

She puts an arm over my body and her head next to mine on the pillow. "It's only eight. You can go back to sleep. I'll just lie here with you."

I roll over and try to get comfortable, but I can't. "I'm awake now," I say.

"Great!" Mom exclaims. "I thought we could have a girls' day! Want to go shopping? Go get some bagels?"

I rub my eyes, willing myself to be cheery and more awake. "Um, sure," I say.

Mom sits up. "Which one? Shopping or bagels?"

I close my eyes again. "Both?"

"Super! I'll go shower, okay?"

"Okay, Mom."

When she's gone, I get out of bed and cross to my closet. It's not a school day, so I don't have to wear jeans to be like everyone else. I toss on a navy-and-white striped tank dress and run a comb through my hair to make it lie flat. That doesn't work; unfortunately, my hair is like a scalene trapezoid, never quite equal on any side. I can hear the water running for Mom's shower, so I know I still have time. I sit down to open Molly's latest email.

Why don't you tell them about Theo? Maybe you'll fit in better at school when they know you lost somebody too.

If only it were that easy. I hit the *reply* button and start to type.

I can't. It's not the same. My losing Theo is nothing like what happened here. He was sick, and I had years to prepare for his death. It's not like someone getting shot. It's not the same at all.

Before I hit *send*, I add something about going shopping with my mom and how I hope Molly's having a good weekend.

In the car, my mom checks her damp hair in the

rearview mirror before she backs out of the driveway. "This is so fun," she says.

I snort. "Mom, we haven't even left our street yet."

"I know," she says. "I'm just happy to have some time with you."

I love riding in the car with my mom. It's the easiest place to actually talk. We don't have to look at each other. She watches the road, and I stare out the window, but we're alone, and she's listening. We're an angle: two rays, with the car as our endpoint in common.

"Why did we move here?" I ask her. It's something I've been wanting to bring up again ever since I started school, but this is the first chance we've had to actually talk.

"Why did we move here?" she repeats, thinking. "Well, we felt like we needed a change. And it's a good commute to work for Dad and me. But you know all that." At a stop sign, she looks over at me. "So what are you really asking?"

I don't meet her eyes. Instead, I stare out at my bus stop. I think of all the kids who stand there with me every morning, scattered points on a graph. They've all experienced something I can't begin to wrap my head around. Going to their school puts me somewhere on the same axis, but I'm definitely not in a position to create a straight line with any of them.

"This town," I say slowly, trying to put into words the things I want to tell her. "The shooting. It's like it's still happening. It's still so fresh. At least that's how it seems to me."

We're driving again and Mom is signaling to get on the highway. "Well, we're no strangers to loss, Lucy. We of all people understand how it can still feel fresh much later."

"Yeah, but this is different."

"How?"

"It's so . . . gruesome. So violent."

Mom turns off the radio station that's been playing at low volume in the background. "I don't think Queensland should be punished forever because of a tragedy."

"I'm not saying it should," I begin.

My mom interrupts. "I just felt sorry for it. For everyone here. Folks were moving away, turning their backs on the schools and the businesses, all because of this sad, sad event. It didn't seem fair."

I study her, now that her eyes are focused on the road. "So you're trying to help? To make Queensland feel better?"

"Something like that," my mom says. She switches

into the right lane, glancing behind us for other cars.

"But what about . . ." I stop, realizing I was going to say "me," and that doesn't seem like the right thing to say. It would be selfish, I know.

I try again. "But all these kids. They're so, um, damaged, I guess."

Mom frowns. "I'm sorry you feel that way."

"I didn't mean it like that!"

"Okay. I know what you mean. But are you damaged? Because of Theo?"

I think for a moment. "No . . ." But it's different. I don't know how to explain that to my mother.

"Right. You're better for it. Better for having known him and for having been through it. And these kids, well, I hope they've all grown from surviving the tragedy, and maybe they're wiser for it, more sensitive. More kind."

I think of the word *kind* after she says it. So far, no one at school has been particularly kind to me.

"But Mom, they've all seen . . ." I trail off.

"The violence? The horror?" she asks.

I nod.

"Did I ever tell you about my grandparents?"

"The ones from Germany?" She talks about them a lot.

My mother nods. "They met in a concentration camp in Germany during World War II. They were persecuted because they were Jewish. They saw so many people die and starve, witnessed so much atrocity. But they survived, and they came to America, and they built a beautiful life together."

It's a familiar story. After watching their entire families get killed by the Nazis, my great-grandparents managed to become—according to Mom—the happiest people in the world in spite of everything they'd endured. They were the most in love couple, always holding hands and smiling at each other in photos. They lived into their nineties together and focused on gratitude, on doing good in the world through charity and volunteer work.

"So you're saying the kids in my class are like Great-Grandma Inge and Great-Grandpa Eric?"

"In some ways, maybe," my mom says, turning off the highway ramp toward the mall parking lot.

"If they're lucky," I say.

"Yes. If they're lucky. Just because someone has seen horrors doesn't mean they're incapable of finding joy or meaning in their lives and should be written off forever."

I nod. I see her point. But I still have no idea how to make friends here.

∞

That night, there's another piece of paper in my room with a typed math joke on it.

What kind of meals do math teachers eat?
Square ones!

I look around again, which is silly. I am alone in my room. 1 x 1 = 1. It's just me here.

I know there's no way this is actually from Bette. But what if it were? What if, somehow, she knew I needed a friend, and a joke?

I know for sure that that can't be true. But again, I write a joke in return . . . just in case.

What did Zero say to Eight?
"Nice belt!"

And I leave it out on the desk, where she can easily find it.

∞

"I want to take the mime class," I tell Mr. Jackson on Monday. The bell has just rung, and the room is clearing out. I know I'll have to hurry to make my bus.

Mr. Jackson comes around from his desk and sits on the edge of it. He clasps his hands together in front of him and smiles. "I am so happy to hear that, Lucy. I think it'll be so good."

I pick up my tote bag. For the first time in I don't know how long, I can feel myself smiling naturally, without having to remind the muscles to do it. My mouth spreads into an arc, like points along a circle. I'm so surprised that I reach up to my face to feel it, not sure the smile is real.

It is, but Mr. Jackson is watching me curiously. "You okay?" he says.

I put my hand down, but the smile remains. "Yeah!" I say. And I actually mean it.

∞

"Okay, so what's with the math jokes?" I ask my mother after dinner that night. There was another joke in my room when I got home from school:

What did one decimal say to the other?
"Did you get my point?"

I have to know where they're coming from and why.

My father is in the adjoining room, but it doesn't matter, because I know it can't be him. He's way too distracted and oblivious to be thinking about jokes like that. My mother looks baffled. The evening sun shines through the top of the dining room window and makes a rainbow on the wall behind the table from the crystal chandelier. The chandelier, of course, is new. One more thing to take up space here.

"What are you talking about, sweetie?" my mom asks. She's straightening picture frames on the wall, leveling up each corner to make perfect lines.

"The notes?" I say. "With the math problems? I mean, the jokes—you know?" I'm stuttering and making no sense. My mom looks legitimately innocent.

"I don't know," she says to me. "Beau?" She calls to my dad in the living room.

My dad's head snaps up. "What? Sorry?"

"What Lulu said—about some math jokes? Do you know what she's talking about?"

I put down my history textbook and watch my dad. His face is absolutely blank. He hasn't noticed the new art on the walls, or the crystal chandelier that casts tiny rainbows on the walls in the late afternoon. Some days it seems he hasn't noticed that we're in a new house and starting over at all.

"I have no idea." He goes back to his book.

Well, it can't be Dad. Math's not his thing. He's always vaguely thought it was nice that I liked it so much, but he's never gotten involved. And it's not like him to leave me notes. He can barely talk to me in person, so why would he go to all that trouble?

I shake my head. This doesn't add up, but I don't have the energy to think too hard about it right now. Realistically, the joke-sharer has to be one of my parents. But on some level, I'd be less surprised if it turned out to be the spirit-echo of a girl I never knew.

Later, I write back.

Did you know that 8 out of 7 people have trouble with fractions?

Because, honestly, I'm that desperate for a friend.

CHAPTER 5

Question: If our school is shaped like an octagon, and it has 8 sides, how many different ways can I get lost in the halls?

Answer: So far, hundreds. And counting.

By the second week of the school year, we're already starting to have quizzes and tests in all my classes. My first one is a vocabulary test in Spanish, and I get a 96 percent. I missed one word—or rather, I misspelled *hombre*, writing *hombe*. I knew it had an *r*. I was just so nervous that I was careless. Oh well; 96 is still good. My mom is always telling me that there's no prize for perfect, but when tests are graded out of 100, isn't the goal to get 100?

Getting the best grades was always a way I could

help my parents out while Theo was sick. If I was doing well in school, that was one less thing they had to worry about. They never asked me to get straight As, but I felt like it was the least I could do.

I'm much less nervous for math class. We have a quiz on our algebra unit. I'm very comfortable with equations because we did some of this exact work in my math class last year, in my old school. I was so good at it that Molly actually asked me to tutor her a few times, so I know I've got this.

We have all period to take the quiz. Mr. Jackson passes out the worksheets at the beginning of the class, and we all start working. I easily finish in about twenty-five minutes, feeling confident as I check all my work.

But when I turn the paper over, I see the extra credit question. *Describe an example of something that is infinite or something that illustrates the concept of infinity. Be creative!*

I panic. At his desk at the front, Mr. Jackson is grading papers from his last class's quiz. To my right, a few rows up, I can see Joshua writing furiously. All around me, kids are filling out their worksheets. Am I the only one who doesn't understand infinity?

I'm practically sweating through my T-shirt and

jeans, even though it's cool in the room. I'm pretty confident I answered the quiz's *actual* questions correctly, but I don't have a single idea for how to answer the extra credit question. Mr. Jackson is going to be so disappointed in me.

I look down at the paper again. "Be creative!" it says. I feel like that statement is there just to taunt me. Like it's saying, "Come on, dummy! Practically anything could work for this answer!" But I've got nothing.

I wish I could just give an example of the Pythagorean theorem or define "square root" or something like that. Something with a concrete answer and a formula I have memorized.

I think back to the second day of school, when Mr. Jackson walked halfway from his desk to the wall, and then halfway again, and again and again and again, never actually getting there. Now I'm dizzy and my vision is blurry. My eyes are full of tears as I read the extra credit question again, hoping that this time it's different, or that this time I'll have an answer.

Infinity, I keep saying over and over in my head. I can't even think of something that rhymes with it, much less an example of it.

"Okay, people, another five minutes and then class is over," says Mr. Jackson. "Start checking your work if you haven't begun to do so already."

I look up, and Mr. Jackson catches my eye, smiling briefly at me. In a few minutes, when he collects the quizzes and looks over mine, he'll never want to smile at me again. I'm supposed to be so good at math!

Five minutes pass in a flash, and I turn in my quiz with the extra credit question blank. I rush out as soon as the bell rings, before anyone can see that I don't understand anything at all.

∞

We took Theo to the beach for the first time when he was two. We already knew he was sick, and his body was already showing signs of deterioration. But I still didn't quite know *how* sick he was or what it was truly going to mean for my family, for our lives. I still felt like everything was going to be okay.

My parents rented this tiny house right on the beach. From the windows of the living room, you could see right out to the ocean. Theo couldn't get enough of it. He couldn't stop watching the ocean.

He couldn't really speak much; the developmental delays that came with his disease kept him from talking the way other two-year-olds could. But he would point at the ocean and say, "Wa, wa, wa, wa, wa"—all the while smiling, the happiest I can ever remember him being, his tiny arms and skinny legs full of energy.

"He's saying *water*," my mom said.

"I think he's trying to say he wants to walk there," Dad offered.

I looked at the endless sea, stretching far beyond the horizon, the motion of the crests of water falling over and over in a mesmerizing rhythm, like a perfect geometric sequence. The height of the wave proportional to the time it took it to crash and recede. I looked at Theo, swaying gently, forward and back and forward and back along with the tide.

"He's saying *waves*," I said, and Theo looked right at me and clapped. Equation complete. I felt pure love for my brother surge in my heart like the waves.

Both of our parents turned to me and stared. "Wow," Dad said. "Sister knows best!"

"She really understands him," my mom said to no one in particular. She looked at me with what seemed like new eyes and hugged me tight.

We all struggled with how hard it was to communicate with Theo sometimes, but I often felt like I knew what he needed. And that made me feel warm and complete, and like I had the best kind of secret superpower. I'd solved for x, and it made my parents and Theo so happy.

Now, more than anything, I miss moments like that. I miss that sense of understanding, of connectedness. I miss being a family of four. I miss who we were. We were purposeful and steady like those waves, then. We were a figure eight, looping around, intersecting in the middle, continuing on forever Now Theo is gone, and the three of us that remain are just sea spray that has crashed against the sand and scattered into solitary droplets, trembling and alone.

$$\infty$$

There are nine of us, not including Mr. Jackson, sitting in a circle on the cold linoleum floor of the cafeteria. A fluorescent light buzzes above us, signaling that a bulb needs changing, but otherwise, it's very, very quiet. I keep thinking about how nine is an odd number. Inevitably, we'll split into pairs at some point, and I will definitely end up the lone integer with no partner. Unless we divide into three groups of three.

I only know two of the other kids: Rosemary, the girl from my Spanish class who wears the owl pin, and Joshua. I say a silent prayer of thanks to whatever force or god or destiny put Joshua in this mime class with me. I watch him across the circle, clenching and unclenching his fists, and wish I could reach out and squeeze back.

There are some kids in my grade who hold hands in the hallways. Most notable are Sasha and Stuart, who, as far as I can tell, have been a couple since pre-school. They're like rock stars here, because, in addition to each of them being beautiful and confident, they apparently singlehandedly saved three other kids on the day of the shooting. I guess there was a closet that locked, and Sasha had the idea to hide in there, and she and Stuart herded the other kids inside and bolted it, or something. The details I've heard are fuzzy, but Sasha and Stuart are still celebrities. Even the teachers treat them with a unique kind of respect.

"Okay, we're just waiting on one more," says Mr. Jackson, moving toward the circle to join us. He does this thing before sitting, hiking up his pant legs slightly so that his knees can bend more easily.

"And there's our tenth," he says as the door opens. We all turn to follow his gaze.

"Glad you could make it, Avery," Mr. Jackson says. He sounds like he really is glad.

"I didn't have a choice," Avery mumbles, but she smiles a little as she hands Mr. Jackson a crumpled yellow piece of paper.

"I'll give this back to you at the end of class, okay?" Mr. Jackson says, tucking the paper into his shirt's breast pocket. Avery shrugs. She looks around the circle for a spot where it is broken, where she can sit. There isn't an obvious gap for her.

"Lucy, Shontay, make room for Avery, please." Mr. Jackson gestures for me and the girl next to me to separate. The smell of Avery's perfume or body lotion or whatever it is wafts over me as she takes her place next to me. I realize that even though I've been sitting at Avery's table for days, we've never been close enough for me to smell her. The scent is fresh and fruity. I like it.

Mr. Jackson begins the class. "I'm sure you're all wondering, 'Why mime?' The eighth-grade group is doing an abridged version of *Romeo and Juliet*. The sixth graders are putting together a musical revue. Why did I choose mime for you seventh graders?"

He looks around the circle slowly, making eye contact with each one of us. I wonder, as I often do with Mr. Jackson, if we're supposed to answer this question or not.

"You kids have all had a lot of words thrown at you in your lifetimes. A lot of talking. Right? A lot of group therapy and assemblies, a lot of conferences and discussions. I thought it might be interesting for us to do something that has no words."

I'm surprised to see Joshua break into a big grin. He looks excited, the happiest I've ever seen him. A few of the other kids are smiling too.

"Perfect for Avery," someone across the circle mumbles. It's a boy I don't know, and Mr. Jackson gives him a very stern look.

"Peter," he says to the boy, "what did you mean by that?"

Peter shrugs. "She doesn't talk a lot. I figured it would be easy for her." He uses his sleeve to wipe his nose. I hate him already.

Mr. Jackson leans into the circle, and everyone inches in a little closer too, as if he's about to tell us a secret. "Here's the thing," he starts, flicking his gaze over each of us. "There's only one rule in this class. Any guesses what it is?"

A few kids raise their hands.

"Shontay?"

The girl on the other side of Avery—long and lean, with skin even darker than Mr. Jackson's—speaks. "No talking?"

"Good guess, but that's not the rule. Henry?"

A pale, nervous-looking boy with light hair and freckles says, "No name-calling?" I glance at Peter, feeling oddly protective of Avery.

Mr. Jackson smiles. "Good—getting closer. Anyone else have a guess?"

He looks around but no one raises a hand this time.

"Kindness," says Mr. Jackson. "Just be kind. To yourselves. To each other. To the work. It's really the best rule for life in general, I find."

I think about how, at my old school, everyone would have rolled their eyes at this—at all of it. At mime, at kindness. And I would have too—it was what you did to fit in. But here, there's a different feeling. There's a softness.

Which doesn't make sense in a way, because no one has been all that welcoming to me or anything. But it's like the kids are all older than they really are. Or younger. Or a strange combination of both? I can't quite wrap my head around it. It's like a negative number. It's there, and it means something, but it's not really something you can hold.

Mr. Jackson gets up, and we all watch him walk across the room to the piano in the far corner of the room. He takes a stack of papers off it but hesitates a moment and sets them back down.

"No, never mind," he says. "Let's start with something else today. Not papers. Let's get up and move our bodies. Before we even talk about mime, we need to warm up."

He presses a button on his phone, and music begins playing on its tiny speaker. It's not any kind of music I recognize—it's dreamy and clear and sad all at the same time.

"Everyone stand, please. And just let the music tell your body what to do."

I look around, panicked. I have no idea what that means. Tell my body? I don't know how to react. It seems like most of the other kids are also frozen, uncertain.

To my surprise, it's Avery who makes the first move. The music is slow and winding, and she twists and stretches herself in different directions to its rhythm. It's really elegant, and I find I can't stop watching her. I like the way her arms unfold, the way her wrists unfurl. It seems like the music is really sending a message to Avery's body, and her body knows just what to do with it.

Slowly, the other kids join in. Some are just basically imitating Avery—though, surprisingly, not in a mean way—and others are doing things differently. Joshua is jumping. Shontay looks like she's doing a waltz. I'm so uncomfortable I cannot move.

Mr. Jackson walks around among us, commenting quietly, saying things like, "YES, Henry. Just go with it," and "I like your style, Avery." When he gets to me, he says quietly, so that only I can hear, "You got this, Lucy. Just take a deep breath. Let your shoulders relax."

I breathe in and realize that my shoulders are up by my ears. As I let them drop down, I feel myself become a little calmer. I find my head feels looser and suddenly, I'm swaying to the music. "Perfect," he whispers to me and moves on to someone else.

For a few moments, there is no linoleum floor, no gray cinder block walls around us. The smell of leftover lunch trash fades, and I close my eyes.

I'm just starting to allow myself to stray from the place where my feet are planted, letting my arms spread to their full span as I twirl around, when I bump into something. Some*one*. I open my eyes to see, to my great embarrassment, that it's Avery.

I'm instantly sure she's going to be mad at me. But before I can apologize, I see that she's smiling. Reflexively, I smile back, and she gives me just the slightest nod, a gesture that says, "It's okay," and I feel so happy I might float up in the air like a helium balloon.

I close my eyes again and just listen. Once more, my swaying gets bigger as the music does, and I feel suddenly alive. Like while I was standing still, I was just inching closer to death, but as I move, I'm growing, bending, learning, changing. I keep my eyes closed, but I don't even think to worry about whether anyone is watching me. I don't care. It feels amazing.

CHAPTER 6

Q: What is the shortest distance between two points?

A: A straight line

After our warm-up exercise, we learn some mime basics, like walking in place, being trapped in a pretend box, and pulling a pretend rope.

"In mime," Mr. Jackson explains, "there is no touching anything. No touching of fellow performers, no touching props—well, no props at all, actually."

"Why?" asks Rosemary. "That seems . . . unnecessarily hard. My aunt is a professional actor and she uses props all the time."

Mr. Jackson sits in the circle with us. Like we're all equals. "Well, I should clarify and say that there are many forms of the art of mime. There's commedia dell'arte, there's silent comedy, performance art, Japanese Noh theater . . . I won't get into them all now, but I can recommend some books and websites for anyone who wants to learn more."

I think about raising my hand to say that I want to read all those books, but I stop myself. I'm probably the only one who feels that way, and I don't want to seem like a goody-goody or a suck-up or a dork. There are so many pitfalls, and I'm just barely fitting in with the other mime kids, so I'm not about to single myself out.

"Can I get that list of books and stuff?" Joshua says. I immediately wish I'd just been honest and raised my hand too. Then he'd know we have something in common, whereas now, if I said, "me too," I would just look like I'm trying too hard.

Mr. Jackson nods at Joshua and continues. "In this class, we'll be focusing on the kind of mime where there are no props or costumes or touching of anything. It's easier in some ways, because we don't need to deal with props, sets, or costumes, but also more challenging because the work of worldbuilding for the audience will all have to come from you, the performers."

Cory raises their hand. "What is worldbuilding?"

"Great question," Mr. Jackson says. "It means setting the scene, describing your surroundings, and establishing the givens—time, place, circumstances."

I wish I had a notebook to write down every detail of what Mr. Jackson says.

∞

After mime ends, I wait in front of the school until Mom is able to pick me up on her way home from work. It's a long wait.

When we get back to the house, I see that she's been cleaning again, and she's added a new lamp to my bedside table. It has a blue-and-white floral pattern on the china base and a white shade. I shake my head. I know it's supposed to make me feel taken care of—I know my mom means well. But somehow, every time there's a new thing in my life I feel just a tiny bit more lost.

The one exception, so far, is the mime class.

∞

I've decided I'm going to talk to Avery at lunch. At the table we unwittingly share, she seems unfriendly, but in mime class yesterday, Avery was so interesting and almost carefree. Like she literally didn't care what anyone else thought about anything. I really admire that. I decide I want to be her friend, no matter what anyone else says. Honestly, I also kind of want to know what the big deal is—why Mara and the kids at the bus stop all told me not to sit with Avery. What on earth could be wrong with her?

Deciding to talk to her and actually starting the conversation are completely different things, though. There's no mathematical equation for conversation.

I stand at the table for what feels like hours but must really only be a minute or two, because the whole lunch period is only twenty-five minutes. My mind is blank. Finally I sit, but instead of my usual spot, which is as far away from Avery as possible, I've left only one empty chair between myself and her.

I unwrap my peanut butter sandwich and clear my throat. "What do you think of mime so far?"

She doesn't even look up from her notebook. The quiet hum around us—the rustling of lunch bags and the occasional beeps and clicks of smartphones—sounds like a rock concert compared to the silence coming from Avery. I study her; she's wearing a different vintage dress and the same gladiator sandals. Her face is expressionless, impossible for me to interpret. But I remember her smile from when we bumped into each other in mime class, and it makes me want to keep trying.

I say a little more loudly, "Did you like the mime class?"

Avery jumps. "Me?" she asks, looking around.

I look around too. There's no one else nearby. "Yeah. You."

"Oh," she says, "I was not expecting that."

"Okay." And we again sit in silence, but she's looking at me now, instead of down at her notebook.

"So," I say after a while. "Did you like it?"

Avery blinks. "Like what?"

I wonder if she's making fun of me somehow, but she seems genuinely confused. "Mime. Yesterday? Mr. Jackson?"

Avery shrugs. "It was cool."

And she's back to her notebook. I don't know what I expected, but I didn't think this would be so hard.

I'm ready to give up and get my book out when Avery speaks to me. "I kind of had to take the class, though."

I smile because I'm so happy she isn't ignoring me. "Oh? Why?"

Avery leans back in her chair. "It's a long story, but basically it's part of my therapy sentence."

I'm dying to ask what that means, exactly, but I don't. I feel like it would sound dumb and immature of me to ask. Kids at this school talk about therapy like it's normal for everyone to be in it. *Want to go see that movie later? Sure, after therapy!* Or *Did you do the extra credit for Spanish? Nah, I had therapy last night.* I went to therapy for a while after Theo died, but I didn't dare tell a soul at my old school. It just wasn't something we talked about.

"What's your story?" Avery asks. She's looking me up and down, but I don't really mind it.

"I just moved here."

Avery laughs. "Yeah. Obviously. Why?"

I shrug. "Good commute for my parents."

She nods. "They work for the government?" And I nod back.

I wish I were the kind of person who could just ask Avery the same question she asked me: *What's your story?* But I can't very well ask why multiple people have told me to stay away from her. That would be rude. So I'm not going to get the answer to that particular question during this lunch period. And I can't decide if it's refreshing or weird that she hasn't offered up her personal shooting survival anecdote the way so many others have automatically.

I look at her notebook. "What are you doing?" I ask, feeling a little bold.

She folds it open and shows me. It's a sketch of a woman with short, dark hair, bangs, and lots of makeup.

"Cleopatra," Avery says. "From the movie? You know, the old one, with Elizabeth Taylor."

I shake my head because I don't know that movie. I don't know who Elizabeth Taylor is, and I've only vaguely heard Cleopatra's name mentioned in history classes.

Avery slides over to the chair between us, closing the gap. I feel like I have a friend for the first time in weeks.

"So Elizabeth Taylor played Cleopatra in the 1963 movie with Richard Burton as Mark Antony. It was before they were married in real life. Either time." I'm nodding along, even though I'm not really following.

"Cleopatra is my style inspiration for the month," she continues.

I look at her blankly. "Style? For the month?"

Avery leans in toward me. "Every month, I choose a theme. Usually an old movie—actually Cleopatra is kind of late in the century for me. I usually choose something from the '50s. Anyway, not important. I choose a movie and create a look based on it."

Avery shows me her sketch pad again, and I see how, with her dark hair and thick eye makeup, she's meant to look like Cleopatra. Finally her gladiator sandals make sense too.

"That's cool," I say.

Avery leans back again. "Next month, I want to go blond again. So I'm thinking something Marilyn."

I'm confused . . . again. "Marilyn?"

Avery scoffs. "Monroe! Where have you been? Have you never seen a movie from the 1900s? Ugh, don't tell me you're one of those people who only likes the big-budget franchises and animated crap."

I put my hands out, palms up in an *I don't know* gesture. "I'm not really into movies in general," I say apologetically.

Avery sits straight up in her chair. "Not into movies?" she exclaims. I look around and see that no one seems to have noticed—or no one cares.

"Movies are *everything*," she says seriously.

I tap my book and say, "I'm more of a reading person."

She looks at my choice of material. "*The Giver.* Solid selection. You know they made that into a movie?"

"I didn't know that."

Avery shakes her head. I find myself wondering how she's going to get her very dark, probably freshly dyed hair blond in a few weeks, but that's the least of the questions I wish I could ask her.

∞

Another math joke is waiting for me on my desk when I get home. Whoever leaves them seems to know just when I need one. And for some reason, that makes me think of Bette again. I can't help imagining that she would have enjoyed these jokes too.

What kind of angle should you never argue with? A 90-degree angle. They're ALWAYS right.

I smile and immediately get out a pencil to write my reply. I don't even have to think about it—I know just what to say.

Why is the obtuse angle always so grumpy and mad? Because it's NEVER right.

∞

"I have to know," I say at the bus stop the next day. There's a small crowd waiting, as usual, including the big blond boy and Dave and Elisa, the ones who warned me about Avery.

I decided last night, as I was drifting off to sleep, that I should find out what it was about Avery that people were trying to warn me against. Not knowing is making my imagination run wild. Is Avery some kind of kid-spy for the police or something? Is she a drug dealer? Maybe she's part of a terrorist cell or a cult.

Dave asks, "What?" and everyone is looking at me.

I fish for the courage that was so easy to feel when I was alone in my room. "Um, you said that I shouldn't sit with Avery at lunch."

Everyone stares.

"I want to know why," I add, even though I thought that was clear.

Dave looks at the big blond boy, who shrugs. Elisa speaks first. "It's not like it's a secret," she says.

Dave shrugs too. "Avery's brother was the killer."

I don't even process what he says at first. "The what?"

"Her half brother," Elisa clarifies. But I'm still confused.

I look at each of them, squinting in the morning sun.

"The shooter," the blond boy says. "Avery's half brother was the shooter at our school."

I don't know why, but I feel as though I've been punched in the stomach.

"Oh."

"Yeah," says Elisa. "So you probably don't want to sit with her."

And just like that, the bus arrives and we file on, as orderly as the solution set of a linear equation. I walk behind Dave who is behind Elisa who is behind the blond boy. Like nothing is new. But to me, the shock feels huge. I'm dizzy with it, like someone sucked all the air out of the atmosphere and

I'm wandering around with only the oxygen in my lungs to keep me going.

My first thought is, *How did I not know?* Shouldn't that have come with my orientation booklet from the school? Or my introductory tour from Mara? But after a while I have a new question: *What am I supposed to do with this information?*

∞

I spend the morning worrying about where to sit at lunch. Now that I know about Avery's brother, do I still sit at her table? When the moment of truth arrives, and I'm standing with my lunch bag at the cafeteria entrance, all I see is an ocean of unfriendly faces. Everywhere I look is a closed circle, sealed by shared experiences.

Sasha and Stuart sit at a table near the entrance, holding hands as always, which makes me think of Joshua, and I blush. I look around for him and find him at the table Mara told me was the "activists" table. Does Joshua protest in front of the Senate building on weekends? But I know I won't ask about that, because it seems super intimidating. I can't even start a conversation with him about mime. Or math.

Nowhere is there an empty seat I can even ask to sit in, except at Avery's table. I walk over there, thinking maybe I can take one of the empty chairs and drag it to a different table and then ask to join, but even as I try to picture this I know how ridiculous it would look. What if I drag the empty chair to a neighboring table and then the people there tell me I can't sit with them? Then what—I keep lugging the chair around the room, begging for a space? Everyone would be looking at me, watching my embarrassment.

Avery's face has been buried in her sketchbook, as usual, her pencil moving rapidly and passionately across a page. She must somehow feel me looking at her, though, because she suddenly raises her head and our eyes meet. I can't walk away now that Avery has seen me. And oddly enough, I don't want to. I'm better off just sitting at Avery's table.

She looks a little different to me now that I know her story. She's no longer the brash, confident loner who loves movies so much she dresses like starlets. Replacing her is this lonely, scared girl who just keeps trying, unsuccessfully, to change her appearance in hopes of disappearing altogether.

I cannot think of a way to start a conversation. I want to, mostly out of curiosity, but the things I want to ask Avery are the things you just don't say out loud to people. Like, *Is it true your brother shot all those kids? How do you feel about it?*

I'm grasping for ideas, and finally realize I don't even know the most basic things about Avery. It seems like an innocent place to start.

"So," I say, and Avery looks up. "We talked the other day, but I realized, I, um, don't even know your last name." I smile and try to look friendly.

Avery cocks her head to the side, considering what I just said. Slowly, a strange look spreads across her face. It's not a friendly one.

She slams her sketchbook down on the table with a force that scares me. She rolls her eyes.

"Okay, I get it," she says. "Someone told you about my brother. And now that you know, you want to go down the Google hole and find out everything you can about me and about him. And then you're going to decide if you can still sit with me at lunch. And, not to ruin the ending for you, but the answer will be no, you will not want to continue to sit with me at lunch. And you'll never talk to me again."

Finished with her pronouncement, she tucks a piece of dyed-black hair behind her ear, smooths out her sketchbook, and goes back to drawing.

"Hang on," I say. She doesn't look up.

I try again. "That's not at all what I was saying."

Avery peeks up from her pad and sets down her pencil. "Oh."

I shrug. "I was really just trying to make conversation."

She looks at me through narrowed eyes. "But you did find out about my brother."

I'm tempted to lie, but something about Avery makes me think she already knows the truth somehow.

"Yes," I say. "And I'm sorry."

"Sorry?"

"Yes. I'm sorry."

Avery sighs and leans back in her chair. "What does 'I'm sorry' even mean?"

"I don't know," I say.

Avery nods, her eyes wide and piercing blue. "Exactly. Right?"

Somehow, without even meaning to, we've come to a peaceful place. We've agreed on something, and I'm not quite sure what it is, but I know it feels good. We are, at least, plotting coordinates on the same axis.

"So. Do you want to be friends?" Avery asks bluntly.

I'm shocked. You don't ask someone to be your

friend like asking someone to be your date to the Valentine's Day dance. A friendship *develops*. It doesn't get announced or predetermined.

And yet I find myself saying, "Okay," and the next thing I know, Avery is talking at lightning speed, like she's saved up a year's worth of friend talk—or maybe four—and she's just getting started unspooling it, like a piece of string she wraps around us.

"If we're going to be friends, there are some movies you'll have to watch so we can discuss them. I mean, you don't have to, but I think it would be fun. I'd start with *Citizen Kane*, which is a cliché, but it's also just soooooo good."

I like the way her eyes light up when she talks about movies. I like the way she seems to forget that there's anyone in the cafeteria besides us. I'm glad I sat at her table that first day, and that I've chosen to come back over and over again. I think I made a good decision. I'm going to like being her friend.

CHAPTER 7

x = extra credit
Solve for x:
$100 + x = 100$
$x = 0$

Mr. Jackson is passing back our quizzes. He walks up and down the rows, placing the corrected sheets on our desks, facedown, so that no one can see anyone else's score. I'm grateful for that—but also worried, because the extra credit question about infinity was on the back of the paper, and I don't want everyone to see that I didn't have a single answer for it. I'm certain that Mr. Jackson has circled it in red marker and drawn a big X over the empty space where I should have had some ideas.

"Overall," he says, giving a quiz back to the kid

in front of me, "I'm very pleased with the quizzes. Most of you scored quite well."

It's my turn now, and it feels like slow motion as Mr. Jackson's arm passes across my desk, the white paper contrasting with his dark brown skin. The quiz lands, and I see that there is no red X or arrow. There is nothing at all written where I've left the extra credit question blank, and when I flip the page over, I see I've scored a perfect 100 percent. But my joy only lasts a moment.

Mr. Jackson makes his way to the front of the classroom, having passed back all the quizzes.

"There was one thing, however, that many of you seemed to struggle with," he says, passing his eyes over us all. "Infinity." His eyes meet mine, and I blush a deep, embarrassed pink. I knew I would let him down.

"Several of you left the extra credit option blank," he continues, and though he's no longer looking at me, I'm fairly certain that Mr. Jackson is giving the entire class this lesson for my benefit. I'm sure I'm the only one who failed the extra credit question, but because he's so nice, he's making it seem like more people need help with this simple concept.

The room is silent. "Does anyone have questions

about infinity, to start out?" He looks around, but no one raises a hand. Probably because everyone else gets it. I'm too timid to speak up. I wouldn't even know what question to ask, where to begin.

Thankfully, Mr. Jackson marches ahead. "There are many things that are infinite," he says, sitting perched on the edge of his desk. "Space is an example that comes to my mind. There's no end to the universe, that we know of. Yet."

A few people nod, and I try to think harder about what it means. I try to picture the edge of outer space, but I don't even know what that would look like if it did exist. All I see in my mind is black.

"Numbers are infinite," he continues. "Can anyone explain that one?"

This idea ought to be right up my alley, but I feel like I'm underwater. I can't grasp it.

A girl raises her hand. "Yeah, like, there's no highest number."

"Yes, Andrea. Thank you. You can always add 1 to any number, right?"

Andrea nods. "So you can always go higher."

"Or lower!" Mr. Jackson adds, excited, as if math is the secret to the universe. "You can always subtract 1, too!"

Andrea nods, and a girl named Madison raises her hand. "Or you can add or subtract a fraction," she says when Mr. Jackson has called on her.

"Yes!" he practically shouts. "Good point." He's excited, energized.

Madison smiles.

Mr. Jackson looks around the room. "Let's talk about other examples. Anyone?" When no one has anything to add, he says, "How about time? Time is infinite. Can anyone give me an example of how time is infinite?"

No one speaks for another long moment. Finally, a boy raises his hand. "It's not," he says.

Mr. Jackson nods. "Sure, that's fair. It's only infinite in one direction, right? Like, before the big bang, there was nothing? And now time is only infinite going forward?"

But the boy shakes his head. "That's not what I mean."

Mr. Jackson doesn't look puzzled or frustrated. He just says, "Okay, Mateo. Tell me more. I'm listening." I love that about Mr. Jackson. He's so patient.

Mateo shifts in his chair, and though I can't see his face from where I sit, I imagine he's trying to come up with the right words.

"Time isn't infinite for *people*. Everyone dies."

Mr. Jackson nods thoughtfully. "Well, that's true," he says. The room is so quiet that I think I can hear everyone around me breathing. It's not a good sound.

Mateo continues. "You can't think time is infinite. No one knows how much time they have. At any minute, you could get hit by a bus crossing the street. Or someone could come in and shoot us all."

Mr. Jackson's face falls, his mouth turning down. His eyes even close for a minute, and now he does look disappointed. I can't figure out what Mateo said that was wrong, though. It all sounded right to me. It's true.

"I'm really sorry you kids have to see it that way," Mr. Jackson says finally.

A kid named Tyler raises his hand. "So, does that mean time isn't infinite?"

Mr. Jackson clears his throat. He takes a moment, as if collecting his thoughts. "Well, it's a controversial topic in physics. But I think most people would say that time, in general, overall, is infinite. Maybe not for any one person, because—as Mateo pointed out—no one lives forever. But there are always new generations. New people being born. And the world goes on. So, yes, I think time is infinite." I look around the room. No one nods, no one is moving.

"But what about the end of the world?" asks Heather, who's also in my art class.

Mr. Jackson looks sad. He pushes his glasses back up onto the bridge of his nose. "A good question," he says. "I will have to get back to you on that one."

Heather shrugs, but I can't help but notice that Mr. Jackson seems different. He's deflated, somehow, as if someone poked him with a pin and let out all the air from his body.

He spends the rest of class introducing the next chapter's material, but he seems distracted, not his usual enthusiastic self. I wonder if he's thinking about infinity, and I'm disappointed to realize I still don't understand it at all.

∞

At dinner, my parents are discussing the new plants for the front yard. Again. My mother is really into perennials, because they come back every year, but my dad wants to plant some annuals. He's impatient for the yard to look good after years of neglect.

I guess Bette's parents weren't that concerned with landscaping after she died.

It's boring, but on the plus side, it's nice that my dad seems to care about something for a change.

"We're going to live here a good long time," my mom argues, "so it's worth investing in perennials. I want a garden that gets bigger and bigger each year."

My dad shakes his head. "But it looks so bare right now, as if no one cares."

I don't know what my mom is about to say, but I interrupt. I'm testing out a theory.

"Hey, you guys, I have a joke." They both look over at me. I don't know why but suddenly I feel nervous. "How do you make the number 'one' disappear?"

Silence. But my dad smiles.

"Add a 'g' and it's *gone*," I say.

My mom stares at me like she thinks I might be sick or, at the bare minimum, insane. But my dad starts to laugh.

"It's you!" I shout, pointing at him. I stand up, and my fork clatters to the floor along with my napkin. I didn't intend to act so excited, but now my dad and I are both laughing.

"What's going on?" Mom asks.

"He's been leaving me math jokes," I say, sitting down but still looking at my dad.

He shakes his head. "Nope. I have no idea what you're talking about," he says. But there's a twinkle in his eye.

"Oh, please," I say.

My mom is looking back and forth, trying to figure out what on earth is going on.

My dad just smiles. He won't admit to it.

∞

"Welcome back to the cafetorium," Mr. Jackson says when we are once again in mime class after school on Tuesday.

I think he must have misspoken, but then Shontay asks, "Did you just say *cafetorium*?" and I'm grateful someone else is as confused as I am, for once.

"It's a combination of cafeteria and auditorium," he explains. "See?" He points to the raised platform on one end of the room. "That's our stage."

I've spent a lot of time sitting in this cafeteria, alone at a table with Avery, looking around, and I've never noticed that the platform was really a stage.

"At the end of this quarter, we're going to have a performance."

This is news to me, and judging by the looks of most of the other kids sitting in the circle, they also didn't know this class was going to involve a performance. I wonder if they all, like me, are feeling instant butterflies in their stomachs.

"Like, for the public?" Rosemary asks, squinting her brown eyes and wrinkling her forehead.

"Kind of," Mr. Jackson says. "Mostly just for your families."

I wince at the word *families*. Without Theo, I often wonder if we're a real family anymore. Somewhere, I imagine Bette's surviving brother is wondering the same thing. Like me, he must be at a new school. Like me, he's an only child now.

"For our show," Mr. Jackson goes on, "I'll add a curtain to the stage and get lights from the high school. You won't even recognize the place. Now, everybody up. Let's make a circle."

We all stand up. I find a spot between Avery and Peter.

"We're going to pass around an imaginary ball." Mr. Jackson uses his hands to show us the size of the invisible object, a sphere with a foot-long diameter.

He hands it to Rosemary, who's standing on his left. She takes it, uses her hands to show that it's the same size and shape, and tosses it gently to Joshua beside her.

Once the ball has been around the circle completely, Mr. Jackson says, "Now you can either hand the ball to the person next to you or toss it across the circle to someone else."

I watch as the ball travels to Rosemary and then to Joshua, who, to my shock and delight, sends it across the circle to me. When I catch it, our eyes meet for a moment, and he smiles.

∞

Dad's working late tonight, so before I go to bed, I write a math joke and leave it out for him on the kitchen island.

Have you heard about the mathematical tree?
It has square roots!

Afterward I lie in bed, worried that my mom will move the note or throw it away before he gets home. She's been watching TV since after dinner,

but given that lately she's been obsessing over install-
ing shelves, cabinets, and "organization systems" in
every nook and cranny, I worry my scrap of paper
will get "filed" during a commercial-break cleaning
spree.

At some point, I must drift off to sleep, because
when I wake up, it's morning and there's a note on
the end of my bed.

Why was the geometry book so adorable?
Because it had acute angles.

I smile.

It's as if I have two versions of my dad. There's
the one who is often grumpy, who barely looks at
me, and then there's this one who is pretty funny,
who leaves me math jokes just because he knows I
like them.

When I go down for breakfast, my dad is reading
the paper; he insists on getting a physical copy deliv-
ered to our door now, and every so often he actually
looks at it—something he never would've had time
for when Theo was alive. My mother is holding out
fifteen different carpet samples for the family room.
She alternately moves each out to the front position,

squinting to imagine how the whole adjacent room would look with that carpet.

"I vote for the beige one," I tell her, trying to be supportive.

She looks at me, exasperated. "They're all beige," she says.

"Isn't that kind of the problem?" I ask. "So just pick one. They're all basically the same."

A crinkling noise comes from the table. My dad's newspaper is shaking, ever so slightly. My mother and I exchange worried looks, until he puts it down and we see. He's laughing. And soon we all are.

Maybe we *can* be a family, still.

CHAPTER 8

Question: If 1 = 5, 2 = 25, 3 = 125, and 4 = 625, what is 5 equal to?

Answer: 1

"Remember at our last session, how we passed the imaginary ball around?" Mr. Jackson asks us in mime class the following Tuesday. Everyone nods. "That's a good example of how to handle an imaginary prop. Same with the pretend rope or being trapped in a box. Can anyone else think of some imaginary props we might use in a scene or a sketch, and how you'd establish their existence for the audience?"

Henry's hand shoots up. "A crutch or a cane," he says. "Like, you'd limp and pretend to lean on something, and they'd know it's a crutch."

Mr. Jackson nods. "Great example. You wouldn't try to use your actual arm or leg as the crutch, you'd make it clear that there's an invisible one there. Avery?"

Next to me, Avery's hand is raised, and I don't know who is more surprised—Avery or the rest of us—that she's offering something up in class.

"A key. Like opening a door, you wouldn't make your finger the key, you'd pretend you're holding one and also turning the doorknob, and they'd get it."

"Awesome," Mr. Jackson says. Other people make suggestions, but I'm just staring at Avery. The look on her face, now that she's spoken up in class, is incredible. She seems terrified and proud and embarrassed all at the same time. But happy. And I'm so happy *for* her. It reminds me of this thing my mom says to me all the time: Being brave doesn't mean not being scared, it means being scared and doing something anyway.

Mr. Jackson tells us to break into small groups and make up a scene involving at least one imaginary prop. Shontay comes right over to Avery and me and says, "I want to do a scene with that key thing you were talking about."

I realize it's the first time that someone other than me has chosen Avery for a partner in an exercise or a scene. Avery almost looks like she might cry, but instead she smiles and says, "Okay!" And the three of us spend the next half hour pretending we're locked out of our house, and we have a huge key ring with dozens of different keys to try in the door we need to open. When Mr. Jackson has all of us share with the group at the end of class, our scene goes over well. Even Peter, the kid I disliked the first day of mime, claps for our group when we're done.

During school, all the kids still ignore me. Maybe it's because I sit with Avery and I'm her friend, like the transitive property of equality. If no one likes Avery (A) but I hang out with her (B), then $A = B = I$ have no other friends. Then again, the other kids were all basically ignoring me from the start, anyway—maybe just because I'm an outsider.

But in mime, none of that matters. The rules are completely different.

By the time I've helped Mr. Jackson clean up the cafetorium after class, putting the tables and chairs back the way they were when we started, everyone who doesn't walk home has been picked up, and I'm the only one left. Mr. Jackson and I walk toward the front doors of the school together.

"My mom has to work till five," I explain, burning with embarrassment.

"No problem," he says. "I'll wait with you until she gets here."

I put my tote bag down on the ground next to me. "You really don't have to." Part of me is thrilled at the idea of standing here talking to Mr. Jackson, just the two of us, but most of me is mortified that he has to wait with me and guilty that he might be late to get somewhere else. Somewhere important.

As if he can read my mind, he says, "It's fine, I have nowhere I need to be."

We stand in silence for a few of the longest minutes of my life. I am racking my brain trying to think of things to say.

Finally, Mr. Jackson speaks first. "How are you liking this new school?"

I shrug. "It's good," I say. And I immediately think of how my dad sometimes corrects my grammar and wonder if I should have said, "It's well" instead. Good? Well? Neither one sounds right. I go over and over it in my mind trying to decide.

Mr. Jackson is shuffling around, looking at his

feet. "I realize it must be a . . . an interesting dynamic to walk into." I stop thinking about grammar, and we look at each other. His eyes are dark and deep. They make me think of infinity, even though—or maybe especially *because*—I'm still not sure what it means.

"Being the new kid is hard," he says. I nod. But I think he's really trying to say something else.

I surprise both of us by blurting out, "I don't really have a lot of friends here." I don't want to admit that, aside from an occasional email exchange with Molly, I don't really have a lot of friends in general.

Mr. Jackson smiles kindly. "Who needs a lot of friends?" he says, looking off into the distance. "Maybe all you need is one or two. One person who you like talking to. It's a good place to start."

I stare at him, wondering if he's alluding to Avery. Does he know we sit together at lunch? Does he know that the other kids tried to warn me not to sit with her? I wish I could ask him if he thinks it's a good idea, but I know that's not how kids talk to teachers.

I look at his coat, his leather shoes, his ironed dress pants. Mr. Jackson always dresses nicely for school, while other teachers wear jeans or sweats. He looks like he takes his job seriously. I like that about him.

Finally, I say, "Do you think—I mean, in your opinion, what if having one friend means you won't have others? But you really like the one friend?" I blush, afraid that I've said too much but somehow also been too vague. But by some miracle, Mr. Jackson doesn't seem confused. It seems like he knows exactly what I'm trying to ask him.

A grin spreads across his face. "Lucy? I think you should listen to your heart. I have a sense that you have a good heart. And you'll know what to do."

It's not exactly an answer, but it's everything I needed to hear.

∞

At dinner, my dad asks how the mime class is going.

"Good," I say. As usual, my mouth is full at the moment he chooses to ask me a question.

"You mean *well*?" he says.

I nod. My mom glares at him. "Let it go, Beau."

"I'm just pointing out that a class can't go 'good,' it goes 'well.'"

I interrupt their argument. "There's going to be a show."

They both stop and look at me, surprised that I'm freely volunteering this information.

"A mime show? You didn't mention that on the drive home today," my mom says. She doesn't seem to remember that when she picked me up, the all-news-all-the-time radio station was blaring so loudly in the car that we barely could say hello to each other. When was I supposed to mention the mime performance?

"It's at the end of the quarter," I say, shrugging.

"That's wonderful!" my mom says. Her face lights up. When she smiles, she looks like my mom again, the one who doesn't know yet what it feels like when your son dies.

"It's in the cafetorium," I add, trying out the word.

"The what?" asks my dad, a lone brussels sprout visible in his open mouth.

I take a sip of water and try to make it all sound more important than it is. "Our auditorium—where the show will be. During the day, it's used as the cafeteria, but it has a little stage in the corner, with lights and a curtain and everything."

"Interesting," says Mom. "It's great that you're

getting so into this, Lulu. It's always good to keep busy, right?"

This seems like a rhetorical question, so I don't answer. Plus, Mom isn't even looking at me anymore. She's looking at Dad.

"Speaking of which," she says, "I think I'm going to get back into raising awareness and money for research." I know instantly that she means awareness about heart defects, research about diseases like the one that killed Theo.

Dad just grunts.

Later that night, while I'm doing homework in my/Bette's room, I hear them talking downstairs. Dad's saying something about how he's had enough of that "fundraiser crap." I creep out into the hallway to hear better. "I'm sick of raising money to save other people's kids." He sounds like he's had more than a few glasses of wine.

"Honey, we benefited plenty from other people's generosity," Mom says gently but firmly.

"Benefited?" Dad practically screams. I hear his wineglass banging against the table. "Our kid is dead, Victoria. How did we benefit?"

Mom is silent. I don't know what she could possibly say to that, anyway.

∞

On Friday, I pass Mara in the hall.

"Ohmygosh, Lucy!" she shrieks, as if we're long-lost friends. "How's it going? How are you liking school? I can't believe we never see each other! We have, like, no classes together!"

It's true. We have, actually, no classes together. What she doesn't realize, I think, as I shift my books uncomfortably from one hand to the other in the middle of the hallway crunch, is that I see Mara all the time. She's extremely popular. She's everywhere. She's like a transversal line, intersecting everything. I'm just not usually on her plane.

I regularly pass her in the hall, surrounded by her many friends and admirers. And after school, when she's sitting on the bench outside the gym waiting for track practice to start. She never notices me. Or if she does, she never says hi.

"Hey, Mara," I say.

"Oh," she says, looking around, as if she just remembered something important. "Do you have a sec?"

I look around now too, to make sure she's talking to me. "Uh, I guess." The bell is going to ring again in three minutes, but I don't have far to go.

Mara pulls me into a hallway I've never noticed before. It's quiet, and we're alone.

"Lucy," she begins, her face serious and her eyes round, "I hear you still sit with Avery at lunch."

I nod. I can feel my face burning—a combination of embarrassment that Mara is keeping tabs on me and anger that people are so cruel to Avery, my one true friend at this school.

"Do you know Avery's deal? I just want to make sure you have all the facts."

I stare at Mara, my face growing hotter and hotter. I'm glad this is not how I'm finding out Avery's identity for the first time.

"If you mean her connection to the, uh, shooter, then yes," I say. I take a deep breath and remind myself that I don't want to make any enemies at school. Obviously this isn't the first time it's occurred to me that being friends with Avery poses risks, but I shake that thought off.

"And I think Avery is really nice," I add, measured, calm.

"Of course she is," Mara snaps back. "No one said she isn't. But it's just easier for everyone, you know . . ."

But I don't know.

"There's kind of an unspoken rule," Mara whispers.

I shake my head slowly, trying to decide what to say. *Listen to your heart*, Mr. Jackson told me. "Avery is my friend. And what her brother did is not her fault."

Mara looks shocked, and I wonder how many people ever disagree with her.

"Thank you for your concern," I say, trying to sound like I really mean it. "But I know what I'm doing."

Mara just stares at me as I turn and walk off.

CHAPTER 9

The sum of the square roots of any two sides of an isosceles triangle is equal to the square root of the remaining side. If the sums do not correctly add up, then it is not an isosceles triangle.

One thing I like about math is how you have to show your work. It's one thing to say that $x + y = z$, but another to prove how you got there.

And that's how it is with friendship, too.

Avery asked me to be her friend ($x + y = z$), and it isn't long before I get the opportunity to show the work behind it.

Both Avery and I bring our lunches every day because, we agree, school lunch is kind of gross. But you can buy french fries à la carte, and we both think those look amazing. We've made a plan to each bring money for fries this Wednesday. We put our tote bags down at our usual table—no worries that anyone might disturb our things, because no one ever comes remotely near us—and get in line for fries.

"The thing about Scorsese is that he has a definitive worldview," Avery is saying. I'm trying hard to keep up, but I can't currently remember if he's the one who makes westerns or gangster movies. But I nod, because when Avery talks about films she loves, it's like watching a concert pianist play a concerto perfectly. She is graceful and light and mentally nimble in a way I only feel when I'm doing math problems in private. But not infinity ones, I realize, which momentarily makes my heart sink.

If I could just wrap my head around the infinity thing, I know everything in my life would be a little better. Yesterday Mr. Jackson gave us a problem set that involved infinity, and I felt lost all over again. I want there to be absolutes. I want everything to make sense—especially in math, where it usually does. Where it's supposed to.

Avery continues to go on about Scorsese, and it becomes clear he's the gangster director, not the cowboy one, and I'm smiling, watching her eyes light up, when a girl I've never seen before cuts directly in front of Avery in the french fry line.

Avery takes a step back and keeps talking, as if nothing has happened. "His framing, in particular, really tells the story," she is explaining, and I want to keep listening, but my mind can't get past the girl who just literally bisected the line in front of Avery.

When Avery takes a breath between sentences, I interject. Nodding toward the rude girl, I say softly, "Don't you want to tell her you were here first?"

Avery's eyes cloud over for an instant. She forces a smile, but her face is crumpled like a used napkin. I can see her trying to hold it together.

"It's not a big deal," she says. She won't meet my eyes. The smell of grease from the cafeteria kitchen suddenly makes me feel a little queasy.

I'm confused. "But why did she just butt in front of us?"

Avery shrugs. "You know." She says. But I don't. "I'm, you know, kind of invisible," she whispers.

I stare at her, not sure for a second if she's serious or not. Is this a weird movie scene she's acting out? Like "I'm Cleopatra?" Except it's "Now I'm invisible!"

But after a moment, I understand. Avery sits alone at lunch. She doesn't talk during class. She doesn't have any friends, besides me. Avery is treated as if she's invisible. Because of her brother. It's the "unspoken rule" Mara referenced.

I frown. "That's just . . ." I don't know exactly what I want to say. It's not fair. But I also get why it's awkward—though *awkward* seems like a minuscule word for the magnitude of how strange and difficult the situation is, like trying to substitute a single integer for a much larger number and expecting the equation to balance out just the same. These kids are always living with the memories and ripple effects of the shooting. And Avery's brother was the shooter. He killed their friends and shattered their lives. How are they *supposed* to act around her? I guess they just don't know how, so they ignore her altogether.

But I also know that's wrong. The shooting wasn't Avery's fault. And every day, she is made to feel like some kind of leper, because of something she didn't do.

No one is more surprised than I am when I find myself saying, "Excuse me," to the girl who stepped in front of us. Both she and Avery turn to stare at me. I flush with embarrassment, suddenly aware that it's been a couple of minutes since the cut in line even happened, and I'm basically the only person who is still focused on it at all. But it's the principle of the matter.

"We were in line first," I say stupidly. The girl is looking back and forth between me and Avery, as if she literally had not seen us before that moment.

"Lucy, you don't have to . . ." Avery whispers. She looks pained, and I immediately feel awful that, in trying to do a nice thing for her, I've somehow made it worse. Much like the infinity thing, I can't come up with the formula to make it okay.

But all that is erased when the girl in front of us simply blinks, says, "Oops, my bad," and steps behind me in line.

I'm about to roll my eyes at Avery, because that was not remotely the big apology I was hoping for, but when I turn to her, Avery's face is glowing. She's smiling even more than she does when she talks about movies.

"Thank you," she whispers, and I feel warm again, but this time it's not from blushing or embarrassment. It's just joy.

$$\infty$$

We're improvising mime scenes. Mr. Jackson has a big bowl full of scrap paper, and we each write a sentence or action on a scrap to put back in the bowl.

It's like charades—Mr. Jackson draws the papers out one at a time, and whoever's turn it is has to act out the phrase for everyone else to guess.

Shontay mimes "driving a car" first, with Peter guessing easily. Next he takes a paper out of the bowl. He pretends to dig a hole in the ground and drop three little things in it.

"Planting seeds!" Rosemary guesses, so now it's her turn, since she had the right answer.

I knew that one too, but I'm afraid to shout out the answers, since that would mean having to go up and do a mime all by myself with no rehearsal.

Joshua does "watching a movie," and Avery does "conducting a symphony." I feel myself getting more and more nervous. It's not like I haven't done lots of mime in front of these kids before, but usually we're in pairs, or the whole group is acting something out together. Getting up there alone feels terrifying to me.

"Lucy, it's your turn," Mr. Jackson says after everyone else has gone. The others look at me, and I realize there's no getting around this exercise. I stand and walk slowly to the bowl of papers, wiping my sweaty palms on my jeans. I pick the last piece of paper. *Eating lunch with a friend*, it says. And I recognize Avery's handwriting. What are the chances I'd get this one?

I look over at Avery, and she's smiling at me. Since I'm last to go, she knows I have her slip of paper. She must be able to see that I'm nervous because she puts her right hand gently on her heart. With her left hand, she points at me, and then gives a thumbs-up. And finishes it off with a wink.

I laugh. All feelings of nervousness go away. I love how Avery wants to make sure I know she's there for me, so much so that she has to do four different signs to express it. That's so her. She will go out of her way to say something over and over when she thinks you really need to know it. It's usually about movies, but this time it's about me, and I'm grateful. I know I'm okay.

I stand up at the front and set the scene. A table, I shape with my hands. And two chairs. My lunch bag, a sandwich—I take a bite. Then I silently laugh, pointing to where the other chair would be. A friend is there and has made me laugh.

"Laughing with friends," Joshua says.

"Eating lunch," Shontay shouts.

I look over at Avery and grin. She's not guessing, since it was her suggestion, but when she smiles back I feel proud and special, as though a warm ray of sun is shining down through the concrete ceiling just for me.

It's like our own inside joke. Not that it's any secret that we eat lunch together, but I get what Avery is trying to say to me. It's not just about eating lunch. It's not just about having a casual friend. We are real friends.

"Eating lunch with a friend," Marcus yells, and I point at him to say he got it. Mr. Jackson claps.

"Great job, everyone. Lucy, nice work."

I take a silly bow and sit down again. Now the floor doesn't seem so hard, and the room feels a little warmer.

I look around at my classmates. It's funny, I think, how mime is all about not touching anything or anyone. As Mr. Jackson taught us, there are no props, and even in scenes with two characters, all the touching is pretend.

That's okay in mime class, but in real life, I wish there were *more* touching. I think about that a lot. I wish I could hug my dad. I would touch Joshua's hands when he's clenching and unclenching them. I would reach out and shake every single kid in our grade for how they treat Avery. Most of all, I wish I could touch Theo just one more time.

My life is a lot like mime. The most important things don't get said, and you're really not supposed to touch most people.

∞

"It's okay," I tell Mr. Jackson after class. "I don't mind waiting by myself." I would hate to make Mr. Jackson sit with me near the parking lot again, so I say goodbye to him in the cafetorium and go outside to wait alone.

I'm not alone, though. Out on the curb, exactly where I planned to sit, is Joshua, with his violin case and backpack.

I walk slowly toward him. His back is to me, so he doesn't know I'm approaching, and I shiver with excitement that I'll get to sit near him.

"Hey," I say, putting my bag next to Joshua and sitting on the other side of it. I cross my legs out in front of me and stare at my shoes.

"Your mom late too?" he asks.

I nod. "She has to work, so she can't get here on time most days."

Joshua nods. We both stare off into the distance, where the sun is setting behind a grassy hill that separates the middle school campus from the high school.

"My mom didn't used to be late," he says, brushing a curl out from in front of his left eye. "Before the baby." I look at him, curious. "My little sister," he continues. "She's not quite a year old."

I nod. "Oh," I say.

"I forget you don't know," he says quietly. "It's a small town. I'm used to everyone knowing everything about everyone."

Our eyes meet. His are green. I really like them.

"She's a safety baby," he explains.

I stare at Joshua's freckles. "What does that mean?" I ask him.

"I used to be an only child," he says. "And then, after the shooting, when I was in the hospital, I guess they realized they needed a safety baby. Like insurance, in case something happened to me. You know, a backup kid." His words swirl around me, and I don't know which ones to grab out of the air first, which question to ask.

"You were in the hospital?" I ask quietly. I try to picture Joshua in a bed, hooked up to machines and tubes, but all I can see in my mind is Theo.

"I got injured," Joshua says, like it's no big deal.

My breath catches in my chest. "In the shooting? Like by a bullet?"

"No," he says. "I mean, kind of. It wasn't a bullet. It was a shard of glass. From a window. Because of a bullet."

I squint at the sun. "That sounds painful." I know I should say I'm sorry, but I have so many questions, and the words *I'm sorry* sound like the end of a conversation to me.

Joshua laughs a little. "Yeah. It was painful." He lifts up his T-shirt to reveal a long, jagged scar across his lower back. "It punctured some organs and stuff."

"Whoa," I say, and a microsecond later I realize that was probably rude.

"Yeah. I was in the hospital for a long time."

"That's awful." My brain is consumed with thinking of the trajectory of the bullet to the glass, at the perfect angle to force the broken glass into Joshua, making an almost deadly triangle.

"Yeah."

We sit in silence for a few minutes. I sneak looks at Joshua. I knew he had been at the elementary school during the shooting—I gather that everyone in the whole seventh grade was, besides me—but I hadn't imagined that he'd been injured. I guess some scars are obvious and a lot are not. No one would look at me and know I lost Theo, but that scar is definitely real, even if it's just on my heart.

"So, your baby sister," I say finally. "What's her name?"

A smile spreads across Joshua's face, starting in his eyes. It's a different smile than the kind you only do with your lips—it's a real smile. "Cynthia. She's really cute."

"You like her," I say stupidly.

"I like her."

"But what was that you were saying, about her being a—what was it? An insurance baby?"

Joshua shrugs. "Like if one of us dies or something, you know? My parents will still have one kid left." He says it so casually, like that's a normal thing.

I realize, like a bolt of lightning, that *I'm* an insurance kid. Technically, I was born first, and no one dreamed Theo was going to be sick, but if my parents had two kids just to make sure at least one survived, I'm the one they have left. X plus Y equals a family. Family minus X just equals Y. Like the word, *why?*

I feel tears in my eyes and turn away so that Joshua doesn't see.

"Are you okay?" he asks.

I nod, but I don't turn back to him. I can't believe I'm finally having a real conversation with Joshua and I'm crying. I take five deep breaths, like my mom taught me. Back when Theo was first sick,

I used to get upset and angry and frustrated all the time. My mom would say, "Five breaths, Lucy. Five good breaths and everything will be fine." It wasn't exactly ever fine, but the consistency of the counting and the deep breaths helped. That was how I first fell in love with math. I like how the order of the numbers is always the same.

When I turn back to Joshua finally, after the tears have gone back into my eyes, absorbed into my head somewhere, he is looking off to his right, where there's an almost empty parking lot.

"Where'd you come from?" he says, and for a second, because he's looking at the lot, I don't realize he's actually talking to me.

"What?"

Joshua turns to me. "Where'd you move here from?"

"Oh. Maryland."

Joshua nods. "Not too far."

I shrug and look away. "It feels pretty far."

It feels like another universe, in fact. This alternate world, where I had a brother, where my dad was so depressed after Theo died that he stayed in bed for almost an entire month. It was a world where my mom was this activist/fundraiser for rare heart conditions like Theo's, until he actually died, and she stopped going to events and being involved in heart defect causes, even though other kids are still fighting the disease.

Joshua's mom pulls up in a minivan. We used to have one. For a while, Theo was in a wheelchair, mostly because he was weak and it was the best way to transport his oxygen tank. My parents had to use the last of their savings to buy that minivan.

"You're sure we can't just use the station wagon we already own?" Dad asked Mom one night. I was supposed to be asleep, but I was coming down the stairs to get a glass of water and I heard the whole conversation.

"Beau!" my mom exclaimed. "This is what he needs. And what I need, frankly. I have to be able to transport him. I can't be folding the wheelchair and lifting Theo in and out of the car, schlepping the oxygen tank."

I could hear Dad sigh, and I sat down on the stairs. "I'm sorry. I didn't mean to make things more diffi- cult for you. I just . . . I don't know where we're going to get the money for a van with a hydraulic lift."

They were at the sink, loading pots and pans into the dishwasher. Mom used to cook all our meals for the week ahead and freeze everything till we needed it. That way, whoever wasn't at the hospital or at a doctor's appointment or at a heart defect fundraising meeting any given evening had homemade food from the freezer. Theo never ate any of that food, but the rest of us lived on casseroles, lasagna, and meatloaf.

"Bye, Lucy," Joshua says, and I jolt back to reality. His mom's minivan doesn't have a hydraulic lift. In the back seat, next to where Joshua slides in, I can see a little girl with the tiniest ponytail right on the top of her head. She squeals with delight as Joshua climbs aboard.

I wave, and I watch a brother, sister, and mother drive off into the sunset. I miss Theo so much I can actually feel my heart hurt. Instead of blood pumping through it, it feels like the waves of the ocean now, surging and cresting with sadness.

∞

"Can I ask you something?" Avery says at lunch the next day.

I nod, taking a bite of my tuna.

"Do you like Joshua?"

I feel the blush starting right near my heart and spreading up to my cheeks and finally creeping all the way to my hairline. I wish I could disappear.

"Why do you ask?" I say, trying to sound casual. I look around at the busy cafeteria, hoping no one heard. As usual, the other kids are involved in their own cliques, and no one pays any attention to Avery and me. We're imaginary numbers. At least we have that going for us.

Avery smiles. She clearly sees my blush and knows. "I saw you watching him in mime class," she tells me.

I look around again and scoot my chair closer to hers. "Do you think anyone else noticed?" I ask.

"Aha! So you *do* like him!" Avery exclaims, much too loudly for my taste.

I shrug. "I think he's nice."

"And cute."

I smile. "Yeah. And cute."

Avery nods. "He and I used to be pretty good friends, you know, before everything."

"Oh," I say, "but not anymore?"

Avery laughs. "I don't know if you've noticed, but I'm not exactly popular around here."

I blush again, this time a fast flash that fades quickly. "Whatever," I say, as much to myself as to Avery. "It's not like it matters. We're in middle school. It's not like I was going to ask Joshua out or anything."

Avery nods. "Good call. My mom says that the kids who are dating now are the ones who'll get in trouble in a few years."

I have no idea what that means, but I don't press Avery for more information. I doubt Joshua would like me back, even if I had the courage to tell him how I felt.

But I've seen kids holding hands in the halls sometimes, and not just super-couple Stuart and Sasha. And maybe it's not a date or true love, but I often wish I could hold Joshua's hand like that. I wonder what it would feel like to have his palm press against mine. Would our fingers intertwine? Would I forget where my hand ends and his begins? Or maybe it would it be like a comforting pattern, his finger and then mine, repeating reassuringly between us.

CHAPTER 10

A pizza has a radius "z" and height "a."
What is its volume?
$Pi \times z \times z \times a$.

"Talk to me," Mr. Jackson says. "What is the story you want to tell?"

It's the next week, after school, at mime. We've each been assigned to come up with a solo scene to do in class, and a few of those scenes might end up in the show at the end of the quarter. I've been thinking up my big idea at night in my room, but here in the cafeteria, it seems different.

"Well," I say, feeling suddenly shy, "it's this girl."

Mr. Jackson smiles. "That is a good start. I already believe you in the central role."

I smile too. "So she lives here, on Earth. And it's

just kind of too much for her. Everyone is rushing around, and it's noisy and smelly and busy, and she just wants to get away." I pause and look up at Mr. Jackson. He's nodding, watching me intensely, really listening.

I continue. "So she goes to the moon. Like, it's something she can just do. By herself, even though she's young. She just gets in her spaceship, and she flies to the moon. And when she gets there . . ." I pause again, feeling out of breath for some reason as I stare down at my sneakers. "When she gets there, she finds it's the same as the place she left behind. It's less crowded, maybe, and less noisy, but she's still herself, with all her feelings and thoughts, and that's the same."

I look up again. Mr. Jackson's eyes are wide. There's a long pause. I feel so nervous. "I love it," he says. And I know he means it.

"So," I say, feeling awkward, "how do I tell that story? Using mime?"

Mr. Jackson rocks back on his heels and looks at the ceiling, thinking. "Well," he says, "maybe you should pick just one part of that story to tell."

I look down at my shoes again. They used to be white, but now they're a dusty gray, like the walls of the cafetorium.

"It's a great story," he says quickly, "and I'd love to see you write it out in detail sometime, with your words, because you have a nice way of expressing yourself. But for this assignment, since it's a solo performance, some of those details might be hard to convey."

"Oh," I say, feeling defeated.

"So how about you focus on the actual journey?" he suggests.

"To the moon?"

"Yeah," he says excitedly. "The rocket ship part." He bends his knees and rubs his hands together, like he's getting ready to demonstrate. "So you get on the rocket ship, right? And what's it like in there?"

I think. I have no idea. "It's dark?" I say finally.

"Yes!" Mr. Jackson mimes reaching up for something. "So you turn on the lights." And he makes a face that shows that it's bright now.

"And you have to start the engine, like a car," I say, getting a little more confident.

"Yes, Lucy! That's good." He mimes starting the engine with a button and the pull of a lever.

"What does a steering wheel look like on a rocket ship?" I ask him. I want to know the shapes, the coordinates to plot, the radius.

Mr. Jackson throws his arms up in the air. "Anything you want it to look like! That's the best part!"

I smile. "Okay." Suddenly not knowing the shape or equation feels like freedom instead of uncertainty.

"So work on this for a few minutes, Luce. I have to go check on the others. You just practice getting your rocket ship started up and the engine on, okay? Figure out how that would look and feel. Try some things."

He bounces over to where Peter and Shontay are arguing loudly about something having to do with a door.

"That doesn't look like a door," Peter tells her.

"I'm opening it, see? Like this." Shontay mimes pushing a door open in front of her.

"You don't push it," Peter says. "You pull it." He puts his hand out, rounded, moving it toward himself, as if holding a handle.

"You can do either," Shontay says, exasperated.

Mr. Jackson calms them down. The three of them sit on the floor to sort through the issue together.

Not for the first time, I think about how Mr. Jackson makes everything feel safe. During mime class, this room feels nothing at all like the cold, hard cafeteria where Avery and I are misfits together during the day. It's the cafetorium, a place where there aren't cliques. Where I can actually talk to Joshua sometimes, even if it's not about anything real. Where Rosemary and Cory and Shontay are friendly. Where I feel brave.

But it always goes back to being the cafeteria, where Avery and I sit alone.

∞

My mom acts like it's this big coincidence, as if she magically has to go out on Saturday night and whoa, what a surprise, my dad and I are both free. We are always free, but I don't say that.

"It can be like a father-daughter date night!" she chirps, as if it just occurred to her. I know my parents pretty well by now, and I see how this is my mom's idea of a setup to get Dad and me to spend quality time together.

But she's not wrong about the need for it. My dad is so removed, so distant, he might as well be living on the moon. Other than the family dinners suggested by my parents' therapist from back when Theo was dying, Dad and I haven't talked much.

Aside from our math joke exchanges, I don't think we have much in common. And he's so weird about the note thing, never admitting to it directly, that I don't even feel like I can bring that up.

He looks up from his book, and I can tell he wasn't in on my mom's plan, that this father–daughter thing has taken him by surprise.

After my mom gives him a pointed look, he says, "Yes. Great. We could, uh, go out to dinner or something!"

I can just picture us out at a local place, struggling to make conversation, and then running into someone from school, having to explain to my dad that Avery is basically my only friend.

"No," I say, and immediately backtrack out of politeness. "I mean, that sounds really nice, but I think we should watch a movie and order pizza!"

Dad shrugs. "Great."

Mom beams. I know that in her mind, it played out more like Dad had this great idea on his own and I was beyond thrilled by it. Mom's future telling of this anecdote will probably involve me sitting on their laps and everyone laughing together. My mom has a way of painting moments in soft brushstrokes and happy colors, and she's so good at it that I think she actually convinces herself that's how things really happened.

So on Saturday night, after reminding us about our exciting plans no fewer than eighteen times, my mom gets all dressed up and goes to some charity function. I haven't asked her about it, but I know from the look on her face that it must be a heart defect awareness thing, because she has that sad, determined, brave look she gets whenever she's raising awareness. That would also explain why Dad's not going.

"This is so fun, isn't it?" Mom says. "You two get a cozy night in, just like old times!"

I try to remember these "old times" she's referencing. Back before Theo was born, and I was in preschool and went to bed at 7:30. I can't imagine that Dad and I had much bonding time then. I certainly don't have memories of father-daughter nights.

Once Mom finally leaves, in a flurry of perfume and her fancy designer scarf she reserves for occasions like this, Dad and I are alone in the house. We're both in the living room, each reading a book. Maybe we'll just keep reading all night, and he'll lose track of the time and we won't have to sit awkwardly through a movie together. But, I realize, if that happens, we would also skip the pizza, and I can hear my stomach rumbling.

Finally, Dad looks up from his book and says, "Should we order that pizza?"

"Yeah," I say.

After much polite "whatever you want"-ing, we finally settle on the toppings. Dad calls and I go back to my book.

"Oh, and was there something about a movie?" he says awkwardly when he comes back in the room. I reluctantly put down my book.

"Yeah," I say, not managing to muster up much enthusiasm.

"Let's see what's new on Netflix," he says. We scroll through the new releases, a mixture of gritty documentaries I have no interest in and teen sex comedies I do not want to watch with my dad. I'm about to suggest we give up and just read when I have an idea.

"Oh! A friend at school was telling me about some classic movie I have to see." I try to remember the one Avery said I should watch first. "I can't remember the title, but it's black and white and she mentioned something about newspapers. And some castle, maybe?"

Dad frowns, thinking. "*Mr. Smith Goes to Washington?*" I shake my head no. "*It's a Wonderful Life?*" I shake my head again.

"Something Citizen, maybe?"

Dad's face lights up. "*Citizen Kane!*"

"Yes!" I shout, and we're laughing, probably just like my mom is imagining we would be.

Dad pulls the movie up in his queue and reads the summary. "This sounds kind of boring, Lulu. Are you sure this is what you want to watch?"

I nod vigorously.

"I've never seen it," he says, shrugging.

Barely five minutes in, I'm regretting my choice. This is not an embarrassing sex comedy, but it is ridiculously boring, and by the time the pizza arrives and we pause it, my dad asks if I want to bother continuing.

I shrug, thinking of Avery and how much she loves the movie. If she can love it, I can at least sit through it. "Let's see if it gets more interesting," I say, and so we continue.

The movie does not get any more interesting, but the pizza is amazing. And if I squint a little, I can ignore all the new artwork my mom has put on the walls in an effort to *start fresh* and imagine that Dad and I are back in our old house, before Theo died, where things were familiar and comfortable, even when we were sad.

When the movie is finally over, neither of us wants to admit it was really boring from start to finish, as if to say the whole thing was a waste. So instead, we both try and find things we liked about it.

"The, um, costumes were cool," I say, grasping.

"True," he agrees. "And it was, you know, very visually interesting."

There's silence again.

Suddenly, I realize that there's something I've been wanting to say to him. And, unlike in mime, I can use words to express it. That actually makes it feel easy, even though my dad and I don't usually talk about stuff—all I have to do is speak.

"Dad," I say.

"Yes?"

"Thank you for the math jokes."

He looks at me—like, *really* looks at me for the first time all night.

And he still doesn't admit to being the sender, but he does smile. And to my surprise, he gives me a hug.

I have no idea how it worked—there is no mathematical equation for it—but I've hugged a triangle. Maybe I'm a line intersecting it, or maybe I'm a complementary angle next to it, but somehow, we've made it happen.

And it feels really, really good.

CHAPTER 11

Question: What is the largest prime number?

Answer: As of October 2020, the largest known prime number is $2^{82,589,933} - 1$, a number with 24,862,048 digits. It was found in 2018 by the Great Internet Mersenne Prime Search (GIMPS).

Question: What is the smallest prime number?

Answer: 2

On Monday, I'm so excited to go to school I can hardly stand it. I want to tell Avery I watched *Citizen Kane*. All through my morning classes I'm just coasting along, going through the motions while secretly thinking up ways to tell her I saw the movie. And deciding how to deal with the fact that my dad and I didn't like it much. But that's not important. What counts is that we watched it. We tried. I tried. I want to be a good friend.

But Avery's not at lunch. For the first time all school year, I'm actually alone at the table. I finish my sandwich and take out my book, but I can't focus on reading. There's a courtyard where we're allowed to go during lunch, kind of like a recess area, but I've never actually seen people go outside. Something is pulling me there today, though.

I don't have my coat with me, and it's a little chilly, but right away, I spot a girl with blond hair sitting alone on a bench.

It's Avery. She's changed her hair, just as she said she did every month. I might not have recognized her if it weren't for her usual sketchbook, lying unopened on her lap.

"Avery," I call out. I start to cross the cement rectangle that makes up the center of the courtyard. There are a few bare trees, a basketball hoop without a net, and a hopscotch outline on the ground that looks like it hasn't been used in decades. Avery and I are alone in the space.

"Go away," she calls back.

I'm stunned. Did I miss something? Or do something wrong?

"But I watched *Citizen Kane*," I stutter helplessly.

Avery stands up. I take a few steps closer.

"Did you like it?" she asks.

I look up at the gray sky and let out a breath. "Not really, if I'm being perfectly honest."

And just like that, Avery bursts into tears.

"But maybe I just didn't get it," I fumble, certain that I've insulted her favorite movie and hurt her feelings.

"It's not that," she says, wiping her nose on the sleeve of her navy blue sweatshirt. She sits down again, and I inch forward.

"You changed your hair." I'm so confused, and I don't know what else to say.

"Yup," Avery says, a look of sadness coming over her face again. "I was hoping it would make me feel better."

I take another step toward her. "Are you okay?"

Avery shakes her head. "Not really. Today is . . . would have been Damien's birthday."

I take one more step closer to Avery. I'm almost to the bench now, and I want to sit down, but I don't want to scare Avery off.

Avery looks up at me, and I can tell now that her real hair color must be something closer to blond, because she looks really natural with it like this. Maybe no one's hair is naturally quite as blond as Avery's current, obviously bottle-dyed tone, but it suits her much better than the black it was before, and the bangs are swept aside so I can actually see her eyes.

"My brother," she says quietly, and it takes me a moment to process all that this means. Her brother. The shooter. Who's dead. Today would have been his birthday.

"Oh," I breathe. I don't know what else to say, so I finally sit down next to Avery.

We are silent for several minutes. The wind is picking up, and clouds are rolling above us.

"How old would he have been?" I ask finally. I look down at my sneakers and Avery's red Keds.

"Twenty-three." We both nod, and there's silence. A million math problems enter my head, all with 23 as the answer: 11 plus 12. The square root of 529. The prime number between 19 and 29.

"Were you close?" I ask.

"Not really," she says. "Actually, not at all."

"Oh," I say again. I remember how a girl at my old school asked me that about Theo after he died.

I just shrugged, because he was barely five years old, mentally even younger due to his developmental delays, and he spent most of his life in the hospital. In the small amount of time he actually was home, Theo sat on the couch or on his makeshift hospital bed, tubes or IVs always tying him down, always a barrier between us. I couldn't get close to him, and he couldn't escape. We were like parallel lines, side by side, and never intersecting. I loved him, and we had some good memories, but I didn't know if that made us close. But now that I've had a chance to miss him, I know I'd say yes to that question.

"He was my half brother," Avery says. "Our dad and his mom got divorced when he was three. And then my dad married my mom a few years later, and Damien was ten when I was born."

I'm holding my breath, aware that she's telling me something very personal. I don't want to pry, but I also sense that she hasn't been able to talk about this with a friend in a long time. Maybe ever.

"Did he live with you?"

Avery shakes her head. "He didn't even visit much. He stopped talking to my dad completely when I was about six."

I suddenly remember the newscast after the shooting. The man, weeping. The shooter's father. How I had to ask my dad what *estranged* meant. It hits me suddenly; that was Avery's father too.

"Do you have other siblings?" I ask.

"No."

Each time I pose a question, I'm afraid it's the time that I will go too far, but I want to know more. The way I wanted to know everything about Bette, who used to live in my room, I feel like I need to know everything about Avery's life before—and after—the shooting.

"Can I tell you something else, though?" she says quietly.

"Of course."

She takes a deep breath. "I wasn't in school the day of the shooting. I was home sick. I wasn't super sick, but I had a tiny fever so my mom kept me home. And sometimes I've thought—maybe if I'd been there, he wouldn't have done it. I know that doesn't make sense. He couldn't have known whether I stayed home that day or not. And it probably wouldn't have mattered to him. But I can't help feeling like maybe things would've been different somehow, if I'd been there. Or at least—at least no one could think that I knew about it in advance, that I stayed home on purpose . . ."

"Do people think that?" I ask, horrified.

"I don't know. They might. They might think a lot of things."

The bell is going to ring in a few minutes, but neither of us budges.

"It must've been hard for you," I say timidly. "After . . . everything."

Avery pulls a tissue from her pocket and blows her nose. "It was like the whole world went dark on me."

"I'm sorry," I say.

"My friends just faded away. Some of them had been killed. No one at school spoke to me again. Ever. It's like I turned into a ghost. I felt like I had died too, but no one had told me. I kept going to school, going on with life, but it's like I had disappeared. Teachers could see me. Adults could. But to all the kids, I'm not even there."

I breathe out again. It feels raw, sharp and painful, as if Avery's words have sunk beneath my skin like tiny razors and pierced my lungs.

I have to ask: "So why didn't you move? You and your parents—to a different town?"

Avery sniffs. Another tissue. "My dad took off,"

she whispers. "Right after the shooting. I haven't heard a word from him since."

I didn't believe this story could get even sadder, but it has. Even though my dad and I struggled a little bit with the awkwardness of our father-daughter movie night, and even though he communicates mainly by leaving me jokes without admitting to it, he's still here, and I know he is trying. I can't believe Avery's dad just abandoned her.

Avery continues. "After my dad left, my mom had to get a second job just to pay the basic bills, and we moved in with my grandparents. They've lived here in Queensland their whole lives, and they weren't about to go anywhere, so Mom and I are kind of stuck. We need them, and they're here, so we've stayed."

"Wow," I say softly. My heart aches for Avery, for her mom, for everyone in their family.

Avery sniffs some more and shrugs, her short, white-blond ponytail bobbing behind her. She uses the sleeve of her sweatshirt to wipe her eyes, and they leave a little trail of mascara.

I'm glad this Marilyn Monroe look involves a lot less makeup than the Cleopatra look did. Having this conversation a few weeks ago would have been much messier.

"I'm really sorry," I say to Avery. It feels like something I can't say enough, even though I fear it means nothing anymore, like it's been multiplied by zero too many times.

"Believe me, I know what he did was awful and devastating," she says. "There is no excuse for it, and it will never be okay. But *I* didn't do it. It wasn't my fault." I see such desperation on her face.

"Of course it's not your fault," I say.

Avery manages to smile.

∞

That night, I send Molly a short, breezy, casual email.

Everything's great, it read. *I love the mime class and I've made some friends!* Which is a little bit of a fib because Avery is basically my only friend. Joshua and me talking on the curb about his safety baby sister doesn't really count, though I really, really want to think of him as a friend.

After hitting *send*, I sit at the desk thinking about Avery. About her brother, who did the worst thing a person can do. How could someone do that? To Avery, to the whole world? All these pieces of the pie chart just don't add up to 100 percent in my head.

I can't make it make sense.

I give in to the temptation to Google photos of Damien. As soon as I'm looking at the search results, though, I get a sinking feeling in my stomach. Seeing his face doesn't help me understand what happened any better. It doesn't tell me anything about Avery that I didn't already know. It doesn't help at all. I close the tab and delete the search from the browser history.

Instead of sleeping, I let my mind wander over to the other dead boy I can't stop thinking about lately. The other dead brother. Avery doesn't know, but we have that in common. I try to imagine telling Avery that I lost a brother too, but I doubt she would think it's the same. No one hates my brother. He never did anything terrible. My loss isn't nearly as complicated as Avery's. It's simply *Family* $- Y = X$.

In the months since he died, I've often tried to picture Theo as an older kid. A six-year-old, playing soccer. An eight-year-old with a mischievous grin and some missing teeth. An eleven-year-old, graduating from elementary school. An almost-teenager, like the boys in my class. Like me.

I think about what Theo would have looked like. He had dark brown hair and brown eyes like mine, so I'm sure he would have kept those features. He might have been tall, like our dad. He might have cut his hair short or grown it long, or needed glasses like Dad. There's no way to know, no mathematical formula to calculate it, but I like to imagine.

I like it because when I picture Theo as I remember him, as a three- or four- or five-year-old, he has tubes and oxygen tanks and PICC lines and wires. He has bruises on his arms from so many IVs. But when I imagine him older, he's healthy. Older Theo's heart is perfect. It works right, it's not broken. And neither is mine.

∞

"You okay, Lulu?" asks my dad at breakfast.

My mother had an early meeting, so it's just Dad and me at the table, and for once he's not reading the newspaper. He's just there.

"Sorry," I say, taking a bite of my oatmeal. "I was just thinking." I glance at the clock, eager to get out to the bus stop and to school, to get lost in the routine of my day—especially Mr. Jackson's class. I need to get back into the kind of math that makes sense.

"Want to hear a joke?"

My head snaps up. My dad is looking at me, our eyes meeting for real.

My dad is trying to cheer me up.

"Yeah," I say. "A joke would be nice."

Dad clears his throat. "Let's see, let me think." After a pause, he says, "What tool did the math teacher use to fix his sink?"

"I have no idea."

"Multi-*plyers*." He raises his eyebrows and looks at me expectantly, grinning.

I laugh. "That's terrible, Dad. It's so corny! That is the worst joke of all the ones you've told me."

My dad laughs too. "Of all the jokes I've told you? I don't know what you're talking about, Lucy. I'm definitely not the one leaving you jokes." His eyes twinkle, and I can see he thinks he's being funny, but suddenly I can't do it anymore.

"Dad. Please, stop pretending it's not you. You know that I know. Can't we just be real?"

His face falls. "You don't like the jokes?"

"Dad, I love the jokes. I just don't see why we have to pretend that it's not you leaving them for me, when we both know that it is. Why are we playing this game?"

My dad looks at his plate. The sun glints on his

glasses, and I see gray in his hair as his head tilts down.

"I'm sorry," I say. "I didn't mean to be—"

"No, it's okay. You were fine."

I feel terrible. I've taken the one thing that was actually kind of nice at home and messed it up.

"I just didn't know how to talk to you," my dad says quietly.

"What?"

He smiles, but it's a different smile. This one is a little sad and a little sorry. "I know moving to a new place is hard. I saw that you were having a rough time. And I just wanted to make you smile. But I didn't know how."

"Oh." I rarely think of my dad as being a person. It's like that rule: a square is a rectangle, but a rectangle is not a square. A person can be a dad, but a dad's not necessarily a person. Of course I know he has feelings—I saw him stay in bed for a month after Theo died. But it never occurred to me that he could also struggle with things outside of Theo's death— that there would be other, smaller things he wouldn't know how to handle. Parents are kind of supposed to know how to handle everything. Maybe he's not a square *or* a rectangle after all, but something with more dimensions than I previously noticed—a cube.

My dad is looking at me, still. "You're so good at math, and I've always admired that about you, Lulu. I just don't know how to relate. About math, or about . . . other stuff."

He stops, and I know he's thinking about Theo. But he can't quite get the words out. I don't know what to say. I'm just the kid.

So I say, "Well, I really love the jokes. It was a really, really good idea." I look right at him, hoping he can see that I mean it.

"Thanks," he says.

After he leaves for work, but before I have to go catch my bus, I realize that I didn't tell him that he could—or should—keep leaving me math jokes. I wish I had said that to him. I don't want this connection to stop.

I scribble a note for him and leave it on the desk in his study.

Q: Where do math teachers go on New Year's Eve?
A: Times Square!

And I hope that when he finds it, he'll know what I'm trying to say.

CHAPTER 12

As of 2017, the average life expectancy of a male in the United States is 76.1 years. Theo lived for 5.25 years. Approximately how many years did Theo miss?

Answer: 76.1 – 5.25 = 70.85

"You can't use your finger as the gun," Joshua says.

Marcus stops and looks at him, his fingers cocked at a ninety-degree angle, forming the barrel of a handgun.

"Yeah," Henry adds. "Like you don't use your hands to be a book. You know? You hold the imaginary book in your hands."

Marcus tries pretending to hold a gun with his hands, but he doesn't know how. "Where do I put my fingers? Around it, like this?"

I shrug, and I'm about to say that we should just move on—who cares?

Suddenly, Mr. Jackson is with us, saying loudly and urgently, "Hey. Guys, no guns. Okay?"

We all freeze and turn to look at him. His eyes are wide and he's breathing fast, like he just ran a mile to reach us, instead of simply jogging across the cafetorium.

"Sorry," Joshua says reflexively.

"Yeah, sorry," Marcus says too.

"No guns, ever." Mr. Jackson looks at each one of us meaningfully.

"Is that a rule?" Henry asks.

"I thought the only rule was kindness," Marcus says.

"You're right, Marcus. But yes, 'no guns' is a rule too. I guess there are two rules, okay?"

And without even thinking, I add, "Or maybe 'no guns' is part of the kindness rule? It's like the transitive property of equality. If kindness equals the rule, and kindness also equals *no guns*, then the rule includes *no guns*."

I can't believe I said all that out loud. I quickly glance over to see if Joshua and the other kids think it's weird I had a math explanation off the top of my head like that. I hope they don't think I'm just trying to kiss up to Mr. Jackson. Luckily, nobody appears to be fazed by my statement.

Mr. Jackson smiles. "Yes, Lucy. I like that. Let's go with that. 'No guns' is part of kindness." He puts a hand on my shoulder and gives it a little squeeze.

∞

My mother has started seeing a therapist again. I kind of thought my parents had forgotten about therapists altogether, as part of the whole "starting over" kick. But she is "back on the proverbial couch," as she likes to say, and that means she comes home full of ideas for family bonding activities and things we should be talking about. Today we're supposed to share feelings. The problem is, it seems none of the three of us knows what that really means or how to do it. So we're just sitting there.

"Who wants to start?" Mom says. We're in the living room—my parents on the love seat, me in a brand-new chair my mom bought last week. It has a lot of ruffles and flounces, and in my opinion it doesn't really fit in with the other furniture in the house, but I wouldn't ever say that to my mom, of course. Besides, it's quite comfortable.

I look at my parents, tired and a little broken, maybe. They're sitting next to each other, but their bodies don't touch. Now, instead of triangles, they remind me of perfect circles. If they'd only come closer together, they might intersect, and intersecting circles actually look an awful lot like a figure eight. Not exactly. But a little. And maybe that little spot in the middle is me. And Theo, of course. He may not be here now, but we can never deny that he existed. Whatever shapes our family makes, however we bend and round out, Theo is a part of it. He has to be.

Suddenly I have an idea.

"Hey!" I say. "We should play a game."

My parents look at each other. They are both not-quite-frowning.

"I don't think that's the assignment," Dad says, nodding toward Mom.

She tries to smile, but I can tell she's nervous. "The therapist said we should just talk, so—"

I interrupt. "*Or* what if we try *not* talking?" I feel that strange smile on my face—that one I don't have to force, the one that appears naturally like points on an arc, and I try to explain.

"Mime," I tell them. "We should try this thing I did in mime class. It's good for when you can't find the words, you know what I mean?"

Apparently they don't know what I mean, so I continue.

"Okay, it's like charades, but we act out an action. Or a feeling." I look from my mother to my father and back. Their eyes are wide and they seem willing. "I'll go first."

I stand up and pretend to hand someone something, and then take an object in return. I mime licking it, like it's an ice-cream cone. And I smile, because ice cream is awesome. And shiver a little, because it's cold.

My parents are watching me. "What do you think?" I ask.

My dad looks at Mom. He shrugs. "She licked something," he says.

"She smiled," Mom adds.

"So take a guess," I tell them.

Dad looks at Mom, and she nods encouragingly. I can see that he really doesn't want to be wrong, and I feel a tug of sympathy. "Ice cream?" he says hesitantly.

"YES!" I shout, throwing my hands in the air in celebration. My mom claps loudly and even stands up, as if giving a standing ovation. My dad smiles.

"Your turn now," I tell him.

My dad gets up and rubs his hands together. "Okay," he tells us. "This is a tricky one. See if you can get it." He proceeds to jog in place.

"You're running," I say, thinking that's just the beginning of whatever he's acting out, but he stops.

"You got it! That's amazing!" He seems really proud of himself, and really proud of me, so I don't want to point out that he picked something really easy and obvious. And when I see that my mom has tears in her eyes, I'm glad I didn't say it. I hope they're happy tears, but I can't tell yet.

"Can I have a turn?" she asks.

My mom takes a deep breath and carefully mimes picking something up. It's not heavy, but she's very careful with it. She cradles her arms and rocks them back and forth, back and forth. It's a baby.

She silently coos to it. She smiles. She mimes touching the baby's nose and giggling. She looks so in love with it that I can't breathe. She looks different than I ever remember seeing her. I barely recognize her face—I don't remember ever seeing those expressions on her. She's completely happy for the moment.

When I catch my breath, I say very quietly, "It's a baby."

At first, I think she didn't hear me, because she doesn't respond right away. She just keeps miming the actions, loving that baby, touching its face, smiling. Eventually, though, she says, "Yes, but what baby?"

"It's Theo," I say. Because that look on her face makes it clear. She's holding Theo before we knew how sick he was. Before we realized he was going to die.

Mom nods. We both turn to look at Dad. And we both see that he's crying. His whole body vibrates with silent sobs.

My dad stands up before my mom's arms can reach out to comfort him. She steps toward him, trying again to encircle him.

"I'm sorry," Dad says. "I can't do this yet." He rushes from the room, and a moment later we hear the door to his office close.

I look at my mom, unsure what to say. She is suddenly tired and dark and sad again. She's not crying, but she looks like she's aged a decade.

"Lucy, I'm so sorry," she tells me, not meeting my eyes.

"Mom, it's okay."

"I wish . . ." but she trails off. *I wish Theo were here? I wish your dad were different?*

"Everyone grieves differently," I say, thinking of something Rabbi Steve told us last year.

Mom moves to hug me. "You're very wise, kiddo." We stand like that, holding each other, for a while. I wonder what shape we are, just the two of us.

"At least he's still here," I say finally. I think of Avery's dad and how he's not even in her life anymore. Maybe my dad doesn't know how to handle his sadness, and maybe he's not ready to talk about losing Theo, but he's in our house, still trying. "And he said 'yet,' so that's something."

Mom hugs me tighter. "But it was your idea," she whispers into my hair. "It was such a good idea. It was supposed to be a game, and I ruined it." We keep holding each other, and she gently rocks me, like she pretended to rock the imaginary baby Theo. And I just say, over and over again, "It's okay. It's okay." Like now I'm rocking her.

∞

The next week at mime, Mr. Jackson draws a Venn diagram on a big whiteboard he's brought into the cafetorium. On one side, he writes *Comedy* and on the other side, *Mime*. In the middle, where the circles overlap, he pokes the board repeatedly and excitedly with the dry-erase marker, leaving several emphatic dots.

"Today we are going to talk about the intersection of mime and comedy," he announces. I'm sitting between Avery and Cory, who both sit up a little taller at this announcement.

"Not all mime is funny. And most comedy isn't mime. But when these two art forms overlap, it can be quite entertaining." He points the marker out at the ten of us sitting on the floor. "Now, who can tell me something funny you could portray in a mime scene, without props or words?"

Several hands shoot up. One of them is Joshua's. Mr. Jackson calls on him first.

"Falling," he says. "Like a funny fall, on purpose."

Mr. Jackson nods. "Yes—we call those pratfalls sometimes. Thank you, Joshua. Good idea." And he writes *pratfalls* in the overlapping section, starting a list of ideas.

Mr. Jackson calls on Rosemary next. "Something where the main character is frustrated, like she's trying to do something that keeps coming undone."

This is what I love about Mr. Jackson. Even though I'm pretty sure that he, like the rest of us, has no idea what Rosemary is trying to describe, he says, "Fantastic! Tell me more!" as if she has just unlocked the answers to the secrets of the universe. But it's like he truly means it.

So Rosemary gets up to show us. "Like pretend there's a candle there," she says. She mimes walking back and forth in front of the whiteboard, and each time she pauses to blow out the candle and keeps walking, only to turn around and see it's still lit, and so, confused, she circles back to blow it out again.

Behind me, Marcus laughs.

Mr. Jackson points to him. "You got a laugh, Rosemary. It goes on the board!"

Rosemary beams. "My aunt who's an actress in New York City always says that making an audience laugh is the best feeling."

Mr. Jackson nods. He writes *repeated action + frustration* on the list and calls on Peter.

"Smells," Peter says, grinning.

"Show us," Mr. Jackson says.

We all watch as Peter does a short mime, pretending he smells something bad, and he's looking all over, sniffing to figure out where it comes from.

At the end, he looks at the bottom of his shoe, and it's clear that's where the smell is coming from.

This gets laughs from the whole class.

"This is great," Mr. Jackson says, and adds *mysterious smells* to the list. "I want us to try incorporating some of this humor into our scenes for the upcoming performance. Audiences love to laugh."

We break into small groups to make up some scene ideas. I'm with Sarita and Henry, and I immediately start telling them an idea I have about a sketch where one of us is a server at a restaurant, and the server is distracted by a fly zooming around.

"So she's carrying all these dishes, but she just keeps trying to swat at the fly, and the customers are trying to get her attention, but she's focused on the fly. And maybe she uses the menu to swat at it? Or accidentally hits a customer?"

I'm so energized and excited I've forgotten to breathe. When I pause and look at them, both Henry and Sarita are staring at me, eyes wide.

"I had no idea you could talk so much," Sarita says.

"Yeah. Lucy is funny!" Henry exclaims.

And by the time class is over, I realize I've been so involved that I forgot to notice the shapes we were making or analyze the numeric formulas in my mind. For a little while, my brain is clear, and I'm just there.

∞

The comedy stuff in mime makes me think of Theo. He had the best sense of humor. That was probably my favorite thing about him—the way he enjoyed funny things. Watching a movie or cartoons with Theo was like watching two shows at once: one was whatever was on the screen, and the other was Theo's face.

Nothing was as beautiful as the way his face lit up during the twists and turns of a funny story, even if it was a show or a movie he'd seen a hundred times. Even when he was in a lot of pain, recovering from surgery in the hospital or stuck at home with medicine that made him feel worse, Theo loved to laugh.

I remember one time—he must have been three, or maybe he'd just turned four—when we were all at home and my parents had gone to sleep, but Theo woke up in the middle of the night. I heard him cry and was about to go get our parents to comfort him. On the way to their bedroom I poked my head in his room to see what he needed.

"Are you okay, buddy?" I asked. His room was dark, but with the glow of the hallway night-light, I could see him sitting up in his little toddler bed, his oxygen lines still in place. This was in a rare stretch of time when he wasn't hooked up to any machines besides the oxygen, which made him relatively accessible to me. So I went and sat down next to him on the bed. He was breathing fine, and I could tell this wasn't a medical emergency. I figured I'd let our parents keep sleeping—maybe this was something I could fix myself. They worked hard and needed the sleep.

It was pretty unusual, too, that Theo was sleeping alone. So often, one of my parents would sleep with him, whether at home or at the hospital. But I guess there were a few months when he wanted to be a "big kid" and stay in his own room, and his health was stable enough that our parents let him.

"Did you have a bad dream?" I asked, gingerly sliding my arm over his bony shoulders.

Theo nodded.

"Should I get Mommy or Daddy?"

He shook his head.

I thought for a second. "Want me to read you a funny story?" When I was his age, if I woke up from a bad dream in the middle of the night, I always loved for my parents to read me a story.

Theo's whole face glowed with joy and excitement. He had huge eyes, and they got even bigger when he was happy.

I told him I'd be right back and ran into my room to grab my well-worn copy of a book of silly fairy-tale retellings.

"We'll start with *Cinderella*," I told him. Theo smiled and I could feel his whole body relax.

By the time we moved on to *Beauty and the Beast*, he was lying down in the bed, and during *Hansel and Gretel*, I lay down next to him, his steady breathing telling me he was fast asleep about halfway through.

As I read about the brother and sister working together to escape the wicked witch, I could only think of how Theo and I couldn't work together to fix our problems. No trail of bread crumbs was going to get us out of his heart condition.

I kept reading out loud long after he fell asleep. Maybe Theo needed my voice to keep sleeping, or maybe I was reading for my own benefit at that point. Either way, I didn't want to stop. I didn't want that night to ever end.

∞

We're sitting in eighth-period math on Friday when it happens.

I'm still new, so I've never heard the sound of this school's fire alarm before. It's an earsplitting wail. But it's not just the sound—there are lights too. Flashing strobe lights. And the hum of the sprinklers spraying water from the ceiling.

One minute Mr. Jackson is writing on the board about algebra and x and y, and the next minute—*boom!*—chaos. Andrea screams. She runs over to the corner of the room and tries to get into the supply closet. When she can't, because it's locked, Andrea curls up in a fetal position on the ground and rocks back and forth, still screaming.

At the same time, other kids are under desks, on the floor, shouting and crying, and Mr. Jackson tries to cut through all the pandemonium.

"Everyone outside," he bellows, making his way over to Andrea in the corner. "Madison, Bajir, open the outside door. Mateo, please help Tyler."

Everyone starts toward the door that opens up onto the lawn outside the school. The benefit of a building that's shaped like an octagon is that every classroom has a door to the outside.

"It's raining, Mr. J," yells Bajir.

"Just go," Mr. Jackson calls as he tries to coax Andrea up.

I'm waiting to file outside behind Mateo and Tyler when I notice Joshua. He's still behind his desk, not moving, other than the clenching and unclenching of his hands. His mind is somewhere else, his eyes distant, and he seems frozen in place. I walk over to him and say gently, "Come with me," and slowly Joshua follows me.

Outside, we stand in a row near the clearing where the grass turns to forest. Mr. Jackson brings up the rear with Andrea, still trying to calm her down enough to get her safely outside. We can see other classes nearby, in clumps and huddles. The rain isn't heavy, but it's persistent.

I look at Joshua. Along with the rain, there are tears streaming down his face. And I finally do what I've wanted to do since I met him. I reach down and take his left hand in my right.

"Is this okay?" I ask him.

He doesn't look at me but he nods. And I feel it, a gentle squeeze of my hand.

"They're supposed to warn us about fire drills,"

I hear Madison say. Everyone is huddled together now, as if we can keep the rain away by standing in a clump.

"It must not be a drill," says Heather, who's standing next to Madison. "If it were a drill, they would've notified the teachers beforehand, so that all the kids with PTSD and triggers could be prepared."

Heather's voice sounds calm, but she's shaking like she's been standing outside in a blizzard for hours. Mateo has his arms wrapped tightly around his middle. Glancing at the other seventh-grade classes nearby, I can see that everyone has landed somewhere on the scale from tense to panicked. Several people are visibly crying as the teachers move from student to student, doing their best to check on everyone.

I squeeze Joshua's hand and he squeezes back. I look at him, his curls wet and floppy on his forehead, his eyelashes thick with moisture, shimmering in the overcast afternoon light. His plaid shirt is soaked and sticking to his thin torso. My jeans are heavy with rain. I want to tell him it's all going to be okay, but I don't know that, so I just hold on to his hand and blink away the raindrops.

CHAPTER 13

Question: If a woman has 7 daughters, and each daughter has 1 brother, how many children does the woman have altogether?

Answer: 8 children—7 daughters and 1 son

It turns out there was a small fire in the teachers' lounge—the microwave or something caught fire briefly and caused a lot of smoke. No damage was done, unless you're counting the effect on the students. But at least it happened at the end of the school day, so everybody gets to go straight home for the weekend.

The next day, I call Avery.

"It's Lucy," I say. Avery doesn't have a smartphone either, so I've called her home number, but I can't quite picture her at home. It's her grandparents' house, really. I wonder if she likes living there. Does she feel comfortable? Does she have her own room? There are still some things I can't ask her, even though we are best friends already. Normal best friends would have long ago been to each other's houses, but the rules feel different here in Queensland, because everyone is grieving or struggling, and—as I know all too well from losing Theo—that changes how you do even the most mundane things. Plus, Avery's situation is particularly unusual.

"Do you want to come over?" I ask her. My dad is working, even though it's Saturday, and my mom "has a million things to do around the house" so she suggested I invite a friend over.

I can't remember the last time I had a friend over. It was definitely Molly, and it was at my old house, of course, but it might have been a few years ago. Once Theo became really sick, we had to worry about exposing him to germs, so guests were strictly limited. I'm nervous and excited at the same time at the thought of Avery coming over. What kinds of things would we do?

"Yeah!" Avery says. "When?" She sounds excited too.

"Um, now? Sometime today?"

"Let me ask my grandpa, okay?" Avery is gone for a minute, and when she returns, she sounds out of breath. "He can drop me off at three on his way to the store. Is that okay?"

I look around. My mom is nowhere to be seen at that moment, so I say, "Perfect."

The doorbell rings right on time, and my mom comes to the door with me. By the time we let Avery in, I can just see what must be Avery's grandfather's car leaving our cul-de-sac.

"You must be Avery," my mom says warmly.

Avery nods. "Hi. Hey, Lucy."

"Would you like anything to drink?"

"I'm fine, thanks," Avery says.

"Want to see my room?" I ask her.

Avery nods.

As we head for the stairs, Avery whispers, "Did you tell them about my brother?"

I shake my head. "Why would I do that?"

Avery's eyes widen and she kind of nods her head to the side, as if to say, *You know!*

"He's not who you are," I say simply. "That's not how I see you."

Avery surprises me by reaching out to give me a hug. It only lasts for a second, but it's wonderful. It's that thing that's missing from both mime and life—the human touch.

When we come apart, Avery is smiling, and for the first time, I notice her teeth. They're straight and tiny. She has a very nice smile.

Avery follows me up the staircase, pausing to look at the photographs hanging on the wall along the way.

"Who is this boy?" she asks, pointing to a picture of Theo at Disney World a few summers ago. He was in a wheelchair, with an oxygen tank, but from the angle the photograph was taken you can't see any of that. He looks happy, without a care in the world.

"My brother," I say quietly. I turn and continue up the stairs to my room, listening to Avery's footsteps behind me. I open the door for her and gesture for her to sit anywhere. She plops on the floor and begins to take off her boots.

"I didn't know you have a brother," she says casually.

"Had," I say, quickly and uncomfortably. I hadn't thought about how Avery was going to see pictures. I hadn't realized that today was the day my new best friend was going to find out about my old life.

"Oh," says Avery. "Had?"

I nod. I try to make it sound easy, normal, like

all the kids at school talking about the shooting and where they were and who died. "Yeah. He died last year. He had a heart thingy."

I immediately want to choke back the way I said it. *Heart thingy* doesn't sound serious enough. It doesn't sound respectful of Theo, or of us, his family, and what we went through. It feels like saying that Pi only has a few numbers after the decimal point—it's nowhere near the whole story. I wonder if the same is true for the kids at school. When they sound so casual about the details of the shooting, are they just pretending? And do they, too, feel awful about how it comes out sounding?

"I'm sorry," Avery says automatically, even though we've talked about how meaningless that phrase feels.

"He was born with a condition. His heart didn't work. And he lived for five years, which was pretty good, considering. But he was sick most of the time."

"I'm sorry," she says again, like she can't help but say it.

"Thanks," I say. I look around my room, trying to think of something else to say. "Want to play a board game?" I ask, spotting my mom's old Monopoly on the shelf.

But Avery doesn't answer. "Why didn't you tell me you had a brother?"

I bite my lips, thinking. "I don't know why," I say. Avery is still looking at me warily for some reason.

"Did you tell everyone else at school?" She almost sounds hurt, and I realize that this is about more than Theo for her. She needs to know she's my best friend, the first to find this out.

"No, of course not. I didn't tell anyone."

Avery seems relieved. "So why didn't you tell anyone?" she asks me simply, as if there's an actual answer.

And maybe there is. "I didn't want people to know. I didn't want to be . . . defined by my brother."

Avery just stares at me, her eyes wide. I see a little glimmer in them, maybe some tears gathering, but she swallows hard and smiles weakly. "I think I know what you mean," she says. I know she's thinking of Damien, even though it's so hard to compare Theo to Damien. They're numbers with different bases. Like, Theo is base 10, but Damien . . . I don't even know.

Of course, the other reason I don't tell people is that it makes me too sad to talk about it, but I can't say that to Avery. "Please don't tell anyone," I say.

"I mean, maybe I will at some point, but I'm not ready."

Avery nods.

We set up Monopoly and play in silence for a while, other than speaking when it's necessary for the game. I find myself looking around my room, trying to picture it through Avery's eyes. The blue paint my mother and I quibbled over, the fluffy white rug that we brought with us from my old room, my flowered blue-and-yellow bedspread that is, of course, new, and that my mother insisted we get, even though I liked the one I used to have just fine. All these details have stories behind them that I know but Avery doesn't. It's like the people at school looking at me—they have no idea about Theo. They just see me.

And Bette. Does Avery know this room used to be hers? Were they friends? And . . . a question my heart doesn't know how to handle: Is Bette up in heaven, or wherever, mad that I'm friends with Avery?

No, I tell myself. Bette would understand that Avery isn't Damien. Avery is not responsible for killing Bette.

"Are you hungry?" I ask a little later, seeing that it's almost 4:30.

"Yes!" Avery exclaims.

"I'll be right back."

In the kitchen, my mom has left out a bowl of freshly washed grapes. I grab that along with some cheese sticks and crackers and arrange everything on a tray, trying to make it look nice for Avery. I don't want her to come down into the kitchen and eat there—I don't want her talking to either of my parents. It's not that I'm ashamed of Avery, and I don't think she would mention that she's Damien's sister or that they'd care. I just don't want Avery to tell my parents we're kind of outcasts at school—or, worse, say something awkward about Theo. I was never sure how my mom would respond to other people mentioning him; would she burst into tears or launch into old stories about him? Either way, I don't think I could handle it today.

Back in my room, Avery isn't sitting on the floor with Monopoly where I left her. She's standing by my bookshelf, holding something in her hand. My heart drops. It's another picture of Theo.

I desperately don't want to talk about him with Avery any more right now. I've already said more about Theo in the past few hours than I have in months. I try to think of something to say that will change the conversation. As I put the tray of food down on my bed, I have an idea.

"I have a secret," I tell Avery before she can speak.

"A good secret?" she asks, and I nod. Avery puts the photo of Theo back on my bookshelf, and I feel my shoulders relax.

"I held hands with Joshua," I say, feeling the smile spread across my face.

Avery isn't smiling. I thought, as my friend, she'd be excited for me.

"What? When?"

We both sit on the floor and I take a handful of grapes. Avery doesn't eat anything.

"Yesterday, when the fire alarm went off," I tell her.

Avery squints. "So it wasn't, like, an 'I like you' kind of hand-holding? More of an 'I'm scared' thing?" She's staring at me now, not blinking at all.

I feel like she's popped a bubble, and everything I thought before has disappeared into thin air.

"Well," I say slowly, considering. "I guess we were scared. And he was upset, but . . ."

I keep replaying the moment over and over in my mind. Joshua was crying, but when I squeezed his hand, he squeezed back. And he said it was okay for me to hold his hand! It had to have meant something.

Avery looks at me like she feels sorry for me. "That's so sweet," she says.

I feel like I might cry, but I don't want to show Avery how upset I am.

"So, you don't think it, like, means anything?" I ask, trying to be casual even though I suspect I'm visibly shaking.

Avery shakes her head. "If your class was reacting like mine was? No, people were hugging and crying and clinging to anyone in sight. Except me, of course." She looks sad for a moment. "But basically everyone else in my class was holding someone's hand."

I close my eyes for a second and try to picture my classmates, all of us standing outside in the drizzle. Were other people holding each other's hands? I didn't notice at the time—I was so wrapped up in holding Joshua's. In thinking that it was something special. That he liked me.

"I'm so stupid," I say out loud.

"It's okay," Avery says. "Joshua is one of those people who's nice to everyone. I'm sure it didn't mean anything. Just don't make a big deal out of it. When you see him on Monday, pretend nothing happened."

"You think?" I say. I don't want to do that. I want to hold Joshua's hand again. Not on Monday, but maybe someday. And I want it to mean something.

Avery nods. "Definitely."

"Thanks," I say to Avery. Maybe she knows best. She's known everyone in our class much longer than I have. She knows how things work.

∞

Avery is getting ready to leave when my mom invites her to stay for dinner.

"My grandparents are expecting me home," Avery says politely.

"Maybe some other time," Mom says.

After I show Avery to the door, I go back up to my room to clean up the food tray and our glasses of water.

When I come back to the kitchen, my mother is standing very still, facing away from where I stand in the doorway. Something makes me stop, and I watch her for a few moments, not moving at all.

"Mom?"

She turns from the sink, and I can see now that she's been crying.

"Mom! What's wrong? Are you okay?"

My mom rinses her hands and taps them on the edge of the metal sink to get the drops of water off. I can't even count the number of times I've told her that touching the dirty edge of the sink after washing her hands just makes them dirty all over again. She doesn't seem to agree, even though she was the germ-conscious one for so long because of Theo. Sometimes she makes no sense to me.

"I heard you talking with your friend earlier. About—about Theo." She doesn't look directly at me, but my heart sinks.

"Oh." I search my mind for exactly what I said to Avery. "Did I do something wrong?" It all comes rushing back: how I tried to make it seem like it was no big deal, imitating the way the kids at school talk about the shooting. I feel sick to my stomach.

Mom doesn't come closer to me. She leans back against the counter and looks up at the ceiling, wiping her eyes. "I don't know. I just . . . It was something about the way you described it. Him."

My mind is racing, my thoughts churning around in my head like my mother kneading challah dough. "I can explain," I say.

"It was just so matter-of-fact. So . . ." she struggles for the word. "Casual. Like it didn't matter. It's just, it was really hard for me to hear."

Suddenly, my legs don't work. I sink down onto the chair behind me. "But," I say quietly. Too quietly. I raise my voice. "But you have no idea what it's like, with the kids at my school—"

"Lucy! Honey. Let me explain . . ."

I can't even think. My brain is a ball of fury.

"You don't have to explain!" I spit out the words. "I know exactly what I said, and I shouldn't have to apologize. He was my brother, it's my story to tell as much as yours. I get to say whatever I want. You don't even know the half of it." My voice is too loud, but I don't care. "The kids at my school, they talk about people dying like it's the weather report. You have no idea."

Not to mention Avery's brother, and how complicated it felt to describe my loss in comparison.

"So tell me," she says, sitting down in the chair next to me, trying unsuccessfully to take my hands. "Talk to me, Lucy. You can talk to me."

I look up at the ceiling and groan in frustration. "No. I can't."

"Yes, you can tell me anything."

I still don't look at her. "You say that, but—"

"Please?"

And I know I should soften. I know I should yield, but I don't.

I look my mother in the eye. "Fine. You want to hear how I feel? I have no idea how to talk to anyone about Theo. We barely talk about him at home, so how am I supposed to know the right words to use with other people? How am I supposed to tell other people how I really feel about him when I can't even tell you? I don't know how to do this."

"Oh, Lucy. I'm sorry, I don't think you understood me . . ."

I'm so furious. I don't even know where all these feelings are coming from. "So, if that was too casual for you, should I have just cried and told her everything on my mind? Like, that it feels as though our whole family died when Theo did? Like I've lost my parents and my old friends and my old house? What was I supposed to say to Avery, Mom? That just thinking about him breaks my heart?"

Things are coming out of my mouth like furious ocean waves in a storm. And part of me wants to stop, but it also feels so good.

"It's not fair!" I scream. "You and Daddy get to go to the same jobs. Hardly anything has changed for you since we left Maryland, except things you wanted to change, things you picked. I'm the one who had to start over completely, without any choice, with no friends, in this town where everyone—*everyone*—carries death with them so my pain doesn't compare."

My mother is staring at me with a look on her face I can't quite read. Actually, I probably could read it if I wanted to, but I'm not even interested in trying. I've uncorked a bottle of all the things I've been shoving down further and further—for years, really—and now that it's open, I can't stop words from pouring out.

"You and Dad act like I'm just this thing on your to-do list. *Have dinner with Lucy. Ask her about her day. Ignore her answer.* Because you only ever hear what you want to hear. You want to know that I'm still getting As. You want to think I'm adjusting to my new school so well. You want to know that I'm fine. *Well, I'm not fine!*" My voice is like pressure being released from a volcano.

I wait for my mom to say something, but she doesn't. She is watching, her eyes glistening, her mouth slightly open, waiting to see what *I'll* say next, for once.

"Dad acts like I'm five years old. *You* act like I'm a grown-up who can take care of herself. I'm not either of those things. I'm sad and I'm lonely and you don't want to know that. And I've been working my butt off every day so that you don't have to worry about me. I'm just trying to keep it together for *you*."

Mom's full-on crying now. "Lucy. Lulu, calm down . . ."

But I can't calm down. I'm crying, too, and I know I've said too much. I can't take back the words; they're out there, floating around. They flew into my mom's eyes and made her cry.

"I'm sorry," I whisper, and I run upstairs to Bette's old room, where I can cry alone except for the ghosts who are always waiting there for me.

∞

Later, my dad comes in bearing a plate of lasagna.

"Don't worry about your mom," he says, putting the food on my desk. "She's feeling a little sensitive. It'll work itself out."

I can't help it. "Don't worry about *her*?"

He looks at me blankly. I stare at him.

"What about me?"

"Lucy," he says, rubbing the bridge of his nose under his glasses. "The best thing you can do is just give your mom a little space tonight. Do your homework and go to bed, and let this whole— whatever happened between you and your mom— let it blow over."

I feel my resolve break. Like my backbone crumbles, and the fight that was in me earlier just . . . leaves. I just don't have it in me. Either my mom lied to him about what I said during our blowup, or he knows but doesn't want to acknowledge it.

He ducks out of the room. I stuff huge pieces of cold lasagna in my mouth as I try unsuccessfully to concentrate on my homework.

He didn't ask if I was okay.

I can hear him in the next room, reading the newspaper and listening to talk radio as he often does on weekend evenings. I think about going in there and using the computer to email Molly, just to see if Dad might have more to say to me, but that feels like it would require a lot of energy, and I'm exhausted.

Molly's emails have gotten fewer and fewer lately, anyway. I used to wish my parents would let me have social media accounts so I could see what Molly is up to in real time, but now I'm glad I don't know. And I'm glad she can't see that I have exactly one friend.

In the morning at breakfast, my mom acts like everything is okay, like nothing at all happened between us. I'm relieved. I want to forget the whole thing too. I guess we've all become experts at side-stepping pain and burying the hard stuff.

CHAPTER 14

Question: What is the only number that cannot be represented by Roman numerals?

Answer: Zero

On Monday, Joshua is the first person I see at school. He never takes the bus in the mornings, and I usually don't see him until fourth period, when I make a point to walk counterclockwise in our school's octagon to "accidentally" run into him between classes. But now he's right here, near my locker.

His hair is still wet from showering. His face is pink from the wind. My heart makes flip-flops in my chest.

"Hi, Lucy," he says. Normally, this would be the highlight of my day. But I can hear Avery's voice in my head, reminding me that holding hands with Joshua didn't mean anything. Multiply it by zero, because that makes it zero too.

I can't even say hi back. I'm so flustered I just keep walking, passing my locker and the classroom I'm supposed to go into, wandering the octagonal halls. I'm blushing and still thinking about how it felt to hold Joshua's hand a few days ago. But instead of relishing the way it felt, I remind myself that I should probably feel embarrassed about it. And soon, I do feel embarrassed.

The bell is about to ring and I've made a full circle around the entire building, back to art class. I've used up the time that was meant for me to go to my locker, though, so I'll have to carry all my books around until I have time to offload some at lunch. My shoulder already hurts from the extra weight of my tote bag. Why couldn't everyone here use back-packs like normal kids?

The fact that our school is a big octagon, with no end and no beginning, suddenly reminds me of Mr. Jackson's infinity explanation. I will never really get anywhere. I still don't understand infinity, and I am apparently doomed to wander this octagon as a punishing reminder.

Out of habit, I keep looking around for Joshua in the halls the rest of the day. I don't pass him again, though, and I'm relieved and sad at the same time.

∞

"Can I get your opinions on something?" Mr. Jackson asks. It's Tuesday after school, and we're broken off into pairs and groups to rehearse our scenes for the show. I'm with Avery, and when Mr. Jackson comes over, Joshua trails behind him. I've been trying so hard to act casual around him, even though it's made my heart ache, and now I don't know how to stop.

"I've been thinking of adding a piece to the show, at the end maybe, where everyone gets to do a short mime about loss, or about a person they miss." Mr. Jackson looks at each of the three of us. "So many good feelings and discussions have come up through our work in this class, and I want to acknowledge that somehow."

"Like a healing scene," Joshua says. It sounds like he's repeating something he's heard Mr. Jackson say, as if he's in on the plan. I look at Mr. Jackson, avoiding Joshua's eyes. For once, I'm not thinking about wanting to be close to Joshua.

"I'll let you think about it," Mr. Jackson says as he heads to another group of students. "Brainstorm a little if you'd like. I'll be back in five."

Once he's left, there's an awkward silence. "But I didn't go to school here when the shooting happened," I say. I can just imagine everyone else pretending to plant flowers and cry while I'm just standing in the corner, left out like an odd number, as usual.

Joshua glances from me to Avery and back. "It's okay. Avery told Mr. J and me about your brother."

I'm so confused. "What?"

"Your brother," Joshua repeats, as if that was the part I was confused about. And he has a look of sympathy on his face, the kind of expression I never wanted aimed at me. Especially not from Joshua.

I feel like I'm spinning, but I try to keep my cool in front of Joshua. I don't even look at Avery. I know that if I do, I'll cry or scream or something.

This can't be right. I asked her not to tell anyone, didn't I? Or maybe I didn't specifically say that, but I thought she knew it was a secret.

"I have to go to the bathroom," I sputter. Grabbing Avery's hand to pull her along behind me, I lead her out of the cafetorium and around the corner.

"You told Joshua?" I say when I'm sure we're

alone. I search her face for clues about why she did this to me. "And Mr. Jackson?"

Avery shrugs. "Yeah."

"Why?"

"It came up."

"It *came up*?" I repeat. I lean in closer, as if I maybe misheard her, even though I know what she said.

"Yeah," she mutters. She won't meet my eyes. She looks uncomfortable, and maybe even a little ashamed, but I don't care.

"How did my dead brother *come up*?" I seethe.

"I don't know."

"Avery!" I feel like I've been plunged into the deep end of a pool and I can't tell which way is up.

"I don't know! It just did."

I blink hard a few times. "I trusted you. It was my secret to tell," I say, and I feel a hot tear escape down my cheek.

Avery rolls her eyes. "Well, you held hands with Joshua, so I figured you wouldn't care if he knew about your brother."

It's as if Avery has slapped me across the face. I can't breathe. I am gasping for air. "You told my deepest secret because I held hands with Joshua during the fire drill?"

Avery nods slightly.

"That makes no sense! And you said that didn't even mean anything!" I sputter. "And why do you even care?"

Avery looks away. "I've had a crush on Joshua for years."

I feel like there's water pressing down on me and I'm flailing, trying to get my head up to the surface. "How should I have known?" I explode.

"He was my friend first!" she screams back. "You've known him for like five minutes!"

I can't think of anything else to say, so I turn away and start walking. I don't know where I'm going, but I know I have to leave. I know I have to get away from school. I don't care that we're still in the middle of mime class. I don't care that it's getting cold and dark outside, and I don't care that I live almost three miles away.

I walk all the way home from school, the weight of my despair growing with every single step.

$$\infty$$

All through dinner, I'm thinking about lunch tomorrow. It makes me realize I have absolutely no friends now. I can't stand to even look at Avery, and I've been avoiding Joshua so much that he probably thinks I'm rude or weird or both. I feel more alone than I did on the first day of school.

My parents talk around me as they always do, their conversation like snippets of a foreign language film I can't follow. Right now I'm too consumed with hurt and confusion to even try.

"There's a new store at the mall," my mom says.

My dad nods. "There's a new book at the library I want to read," he says, as if that's somehow related to what she just said. X does not equal Y

I just look back and forth between them, my head swimming with sadness. They don't ask how my day was. That's good, though, because I'm a terrible liar. As soon as I've eaten enough to avoid comments from them, I escape up to my/Bette's room and bury my head under the covers. I sleep like that, in my clothes, my head completely under. Forcing myself to sleep seems like the only way to stop the hurting.

∞

I have the Theo nightmare. It's this dream I used to have all the time right after he died. I told it to the family therapist we all saw for a few months after his death, and the dream stopped. I haven't actually thought about it since we moved to Queensland. But it's back, and at first it's just like I remember it.

Theo is at the ocean. First he's running up to the edge. The waves lap against his tiny feet. He runs in, deeper and deeper. I call to him to come back, but by this point he's gone. I run in after him and sink my head under the water to look around, but I can't see anything.

Usually that's where the dream ends. The therapist, Dr. Mattejat, said it represents my feeling of helplessness about Theo's death. I wanted to say, "Duh!" but I guess you don't say that to therapists.

This time, though, the dream continues. And now Bette is there, swimming next to me in the ocean, but it seems like she can breathe underwater. I can't, so I try to get back up to the surface, desperate to stick my head out and catch my breath. But the waves keep pulling me under, deeper and deeper, and I'm running out of air.

Bette is just smiling, looking at me as if nothing is wrong. My lungs feel like they're going to burst. I try and try to find the top of the water, but I can't.

I wake up gasping. I sit up in my bed, taking

huge gulps of air. My face is all wet—I'm not sure if I was crying or sweating while having the dream. At least it's over now.

Once my breathing has returned to normal, I lie back down and stare at the ceiling. What would Dr. Mattejat say now? That Bette and Theo are friends in heaven? But I don't know if I believe in heaven. I used to kind of believe in ghosts, but that's not the same thing. And I don't know what I believe anymore.

Too many questions, and there's no algebraic formula to solve any of them. I close my eyes and try to fall back asleep. It takes a long time, and when I wake again in the morning, it feels like I didn't sleep at all.

My dad has left a math joke for me on my desk— now in his handwriting, instead of typed out—and I barely even laugh.

How many seconds are there in a year?
12: January 2nd, February 2nd, March 2nd . . .

At breakfast, I smile and thank him for the joke, as if there's nothing else on my mind.

After a minute or so, Dad says, "You're not eating much. Everything okay?"

If he'd said this yesterday, I might've completely

broken down. But today I just feel so tired, so heavy, that all I can do is look at him across the table and say, "No, Dad. Everything is not okay. Can't you see that?"

He looks like I've slapped him. "Honey. I—is there something I can do? Something you want to talk about?"

And maybe it's because I can't begin to explain everything that's happened with Avery, or maybe it's because of the dream I had last night, but what I say is, "I wish we talked about Theo more."

And Dad bursts into tears.

I just sit there, with a hollowness inside me that won't let me think of anything to say or do. My physical body feels numb but my insides still hurt.

"I know," he says after a minute, swiping at his eyes. "I'm sorry. I'm—I'm going to try. Soon. I promise."

Which doesn't make me feel better, necessarily, but at least it's one variable I can subtract from the equations swimming in my brain. One less unknown integer I've been carrying around, waiting for someone to solve for. One less unsaid thing to keep bottled up.

CHAPTER 15

Earth's circumference is 24,901 miles. The arm span of the average human is 5.4 feet. How many people would need to hold hands to go completely around Earth at the equator?

Answer: 24,901 miles = 131,477,280 feet, so 131,477,280 feet ÷ 5.4 feet = 24,347,645 people

Mr. Jackson finds me at my locker before first period.

"Lucy," he says, "are you okay? We were worried yesterday when you left."

I nod, hoping he can't tell how puffy my eyes are from a night of sobbing.

"Avery told me you were feeling sick." He studies me.

I nod again.

"Next time," he says quietly, "if you're not feeling well, can you come tell me? Instead of just taking off?"

I feel like I can't speak, so I nod a third time.

"Luce, are you sure everything's okay?"

I don't move. I have no idea what to say, and I cannot nod one more time. The warning bell rings.

"Can you come talk to me at lunch?" Mr. Jackson asks gently.

My head jerks up. This is perfect, because I won't have anywhere to sit at lunchtime anyway. Now I can avoid the cafeteria altogether. "Yes," I tell him. "I'll be there."

I drift silently through my classes, and by the time I get to Mr. Jackson's room at lunch, it feels like days have passed instead of hours. I feel heavy, like I'm dragging a thousand pounds of feelings around with me. I keep looking at the faces floating past me, realizing that I am no closer to being happy or to fitting in than I was more than two months ago when school started. Mime class was my saving grace, and now it's ruined for me. I'm angry at Avery, embarrassed around Joshua, and certain that I've disappointed Mr. Jackson. I would skip talking to him now if I had any other place I could go.

"Lucy," he says when I open the door. He comes over and closes it again behind me. "I'm so glad you came."

I shrug and slump down at a desk in the back of the room. Sitting down at one of the desks next to me, Mr. Jackson takes out a brown paper lunch bag, just like mine, and unwraps a sandwich.

"Go ahead." He gestures for me to do the same.

"Thanks," I say. I miserably take a bite of my peanut butter and jelly, but it feels like sand in my mouth. Nothing has tasted or felt right since yesterday.

"Lucy, I've been racking my brain since you took off yesterday, trying to figure out what it was that upset you so much. And I could sit here and guess, but I think it would be easier if you just told me."

I stare at him blankly.

"You don't have to, but you might feel better. And I promise I can keep a secret."

At those words, I burst into tears.

"That's the thing," I sob as my whole brain spills out. "Avery wasn't supposed to tell anyone about my brother."

"Ah." Mr. Jackson nods, and I can see from his face that he understands. I love him for that, and I'm grateful that at least one thing about school is still good. Too bad Mr. Jackson can't be my friend.

"I told her in confidence," I hiccup-sob. "I didn't want anyone else to know. It's hard to explain why—I just wasn't comfortable telling people yet, and . . ."

"And she told me, and Joshua, your secret."

I nod. Mr. Jackson hands me his paper napkin and I blow my nose on it, noisily and unselfconsciously.

"I have to be honest," he says after a while. "I always knew about your brother. It's in your school file."

My breath hitches. "Oh," I say. I don't know why that never occurred to me. "But you never treated me like you knew," I say slowly. "You didn't treat me like someone who lost her brother."

Mr. Jackson smiles. "I try to just treat you like you. Like the person you want to be, and the person I see you wanting to grow into."

I take a sip of my water and try to understand. Solve for X. "But I have no idea who I want to be."

He chuckles softly. "Well, that's okay. It's a hard thing to know, and it changes throughout your life. I think it's something we're all constantly working on."

"Oh." I look around the empty classroom, algebraic formulas still on the chalkboard from the last class, and try to imagine that Mr. Jackson is a real person, outside of the school. It's hard to picture.

"And Lucy," he says, serious again, "I truly am sorry, both about your loss and about the fact that Avery did something that betrayed your trust."

I start to cry again. "She's my only friend." X minus 1 is a negative number.

"Well, I don't know about that. It seems like all the kids in mime like you. I'm sure they would all call you a friend."

I roll my eyes. "I don't know."

"You're right," he says honestly. "I don't know all the ins and outs of the social scene here, but I see you. I see how you listen and how you care. I see how you walked so bravely into what I think we can all agree is a really complex situation with this particular class of students and the traumas they've survived. And I see you observing and trying really hard to be part of the community in a way that works for everyone."

"Really?" I say. I can't keep myself from smiling a little bit. The way Mr. Jackson says it makes me sound pretty cool.

"And I see how you've befriended Avery. Man, that made me so happy to see." He immediately puts his hands up in front of him. "Not that you have to forgive her. I know she hurt you, and that hurt is real and valid. But I noticed that the two of you seemed to be getting to be close friends, and I'd hate to see you both lose each other. Especially her—I think you're such a great influence on Avery."

"Me?" I say, surprised again by Mr. Jackson's take on this.

He nods. "Again, absolutely no pressure from me. If you don't feel comfortable around her at this point, you have every right to step back from her. But I know from my own experiences that even the people who love us the most sometimes break our hearts. And a lot of times, they don't mean to. Or they don't realize how much they've hurt us. Or they don't think before speaking and, maybe, really regret it later."

I study Mr. Jackson's face as he talks, wondering who broke his heart.

The phrase *break our hearts* always sticks out for me whenever I hear it. Theo was born with a broken heart. Literally. And as a result, he broke all of ours. I know Theo didn't mean to, and it's not his fault that my parents and I are hurting now as a result.

Of course, Theo dying isn't remotely the same as Avery choosing to break a promise to me. But maybe Mr. Jackson's right. Maybe she didn't realize how much it would hurt me.

"So," I say slowly, thinking out loud, "if I do want to forgive Avery . . ." But I trail off because I don't know what else to say. I don't even know the questions I want to ask, let alone their answers.

"Okay, yeah. So, you mean, what would that look like? How would it work?" It's like Mr. Jackson knows how to open the doors for me, but he never puts words in my mouth. He just lets me figure it out. He writes the equations but he lets me solve them.

Suddenly I know what I want to ask. "How can I ever trust her again?"

His mouth is full of food, but he nods, and I think I see a smile in his eyes. "It's not easy," he says once he's swallowed. "There's no one right answer. But I think it's kind of like an improv, like we did in mime? Where you just dive in. You start, and hope you figure it out as you go."

I nod. The bell rings to tell us that lunch is over. I feel like another whole year has gone by in the twenty minutes I've spent with Mr. Jackson. I get up, putting the uneaten remains of my lunch back in the paper bag. I start to walk toward the door.

"And Lucy?"

I turn around to face him.

"I actually think the hardest thing will be getting Avery to forgive herself." He shrugs. "Just a guess, but I would imagine she's taking this pretty hard. I would hope that she really regrets the whole thing. And maybe she's learned from it?"

I nod. "Okay."

"Thanks for having lunch with me," Mr. Jackson says. He's still sitting at the student desk. It's too small for him, and from where I stand, he looks like a giant trying to fold his long, grown-up legs beneath it.

"Thanks for inviting me." I feel like a huge weight has been lifted off my chest. I'm not necessarily ready to forgive Avery. It's just nice to know that it's an option. I don't have to lose my friend.

∞

My dad is at a late work meeting, so it's just Mom and me at dinner. Usually she would try to make conversation, like she does when Dad is there, except even more focused on me and on school. But tonight she's very, very quiet.

For some reason, instead of ignoring this and just

trying to finish eating as quickly as possible, I ask if she's okay.

"Of course," Mom says, her head snapping up, eyes bright and a big smile pasted on her face.

"Okay," I say, not really believing it. She answered the question automatically, like I'd said, "What's 2 plus 2?" and we all know it's 4, except, today, maybe it's somehow not.

"Actually, I'm tired," she says after a while.

"Me too," I say. We go back to eating in silence, but I keep looking up at her, waiting for her to say more. I watch her cut her food into tiny pieces and eat each one slowly, chewing carefully.

"Do you remember when you asked me why we moved here?" she says finally.

I nod, thinking back to that day in the car. It feels like years ago.

Mom puts her utensils down. "I thought we all needed a change. I guess I thought that was going to fix everything." She looks up at the ceiling. "I didn't think enough about how it was going to be hard for you, and I've been wanting to say . . . that I'm sorry."

I'm so surprised that I can barely swallow the bite of fish in my mouth. It goes down the wrong pipe, and I cough. My mom fusses around me, patting my back and making sure I drink water. When she's sure I'm okay, she sits again.

"Thank you," I say. And while I am saying thanks about her help with the water and all, I also mean it about her apology. I look at her, hoping she knows that. I'm not sure she does.

My mother looks down at her hands. She twists them, weaving her fingers in and out. It makes me think of Joshua.

"I think," she says slowly, "on some level, I wanted to blend in. With other people who lost a child." She looks up at me and I see tears in her eyes. "I was tired of people avoiding me, of the looks of pity in the grocery store. Here, we fit right in. Or I thought we would."

I nod slowly, absorbing this. "But it's different. The shooting."

She smiles sadly. "Of course. Like you told me, every loss is different."

"But Mom. You've obviously been trying so hard to start fresh—like with the redecorating, and the new house, gardening, everything. Have you and Dad even told anyone here about Theo?"

Her shoulders slump. I realize I haven't heard

either of my parents talk about meeting people in Queensland—neighbors, other parents, random people in the store. Dad's always at work, and Mom's been piling fundraising and therapy on top of her own job. When would they have time to make friends?

"I didn't really think that part through either. How we would make it known to people. It's not something you can just announce when you introduce yourself. I think subconsciously I hoped that people would sense it just by looking at us, that there'd be an unspoken understanding. Which is completely unrealistic, of course."

"And when I told Avery . . ."

She crosses over to me and wraps me in the kind of hug I remember from when I was a little kid, when she seemed big enough to cover me completely in her body and protect me from the world.

"I'm really sorry about how I acted then. I was so involved in my own feelings, I wasn't thinking of yours. I didn't handle that so well."

"It's okay," I tell her, breathing her in. And it is. She's my mother, and I feel a kind of love for her I can't illustrate with numerical equations or put into words. And since I can't, I don't say anything else.

My mom leads me over to the sofa, where we both sit. "I'm afraid I—we, your dad and I—we haven't handled a lot of this well. The past year. Or maybe even more."

"It's okay, Mom."

"No," she says forcefully. For a moment I'm worried she's mad at me, until I realize that she's mad at herself. "It's not okay. Lucy, what you said the other day . . . you were right. For so long I've been counting on you to be the easy kid, the one who could take care of herself, the one I didn't have to worry about. But that's so unfair of me."

I don't know what to say to that.

Mom keeps going. "I want you to know that I see how amazing you are—how hard you work, how thoughtful and generous you are. I'm so proud of you, but I also feel like I had nothing to do with it. You're blossoming, but I know you're also hurting. And I'm so sorry that I've never really thought about it from your perspective. I thought that by buying you nice things and decorating your room . . ."

She trails off, but I just watch her, hoping she'll finish what she started to say. She's staring off into the distance, and I wish I could map her mind like a math problem, put all her thoughts on a graph, and analyze them to make a recognizable shape.

"I've been pretty confused," she admits. "I hope you can forgive me and be patient with me. Still figuring out how to do this grieving thing."

"It seemed to me like you and Dad had it all figured out. Moving here, moving on."

She smooths some hair out of my eyes. "Oh, honey. I don't want to scare you, but no one has anything all figured out. We are all always doing everything for the first time. I may be a grown-up, but I'm the mom of a twelve-year-old for the first time. A forty-four-year-old woman for the first time. You know what I mean?"

I nod, mesmerized by the feeling of her hand smoothing my forehead over and over, like ocean waves of love, figure eights, and childhood memories. I study my mother: her bright, wet eyes and her thick hair. Her tiredness, her sadness. I'm not thinking of numbers or creating equations with them, even though she mentioned our ages—I'm just seeing her as a person. And I realize that someday, she will get old.

"Grown-ups make mistakes," she says. "We are still figuring things out all the time. I'm sorry for that."

"Don't be," I say, leaning my head against her chest. She's warm and surprisingly bony. I remember her being softer or fuller. And bigger. Now I'm almost as tall as she is. And for the first time I notice a few strands of gray in her hair. It's funny what you can see when you're not just trying to plug everything into a mathematical formula. I feel the air in the room settle. A sense of understanding, of a certain kind of comfort, wraps around us like a blanket.

"I love you, pumpkin," she says. She hasn't called me by that nickname since preschool.

"I love you too," I say. Followed by "I miss Theo."

I think it's the first time any of us has actually said it out loud. Through all those therapy sessions and all those dinners, it just seemed obvious—and, at the same time, too overwhelming to admit. But now that I've spoken the words, I feel something relax inside me.

Mom presses a kiss to my forehead. "I miss him too," she says.

CHAPTER 16

If "i" is of lesser value than 3 times u, then i<3u
(I love you)

For the most part, it's easy enough to avoid Avery at school, since we don't have any classes together. Of course, the big problem is lunch. There's nowhere else for me to sit, and I can't hide in Mr. Jackson's room for the rest of the year. So on Thursday, armed with a book, I quietly plop my bag down at our usual table. I'm back to sitting as far away from Avery as possible, like we're the two points on a diameter.

It's the first time we've seen each other since our fight, and I'm expecting to be freshly angry.

But when I see her across the table, before she sees me, something inside me melts a little bit. Because it's Avery. Because of all I know now. She is surrounded by empty chairs, and I imagine for a second that each one is occupied by a ghost of some kind—a friend who was killed in the shooting, or her brother, or her father who took off.

Avery is scribbling in her sketchbook, and she doesn't see me watching her. She hasn't heard me approach.

"I'm only sitting here because I have nowhere else to sit," I announce, and her head snaps up.

"Oh, Lucy," she says, standing up. Her face crumples, and she starts to cry. "I'm so sorry. I—"

I sit down in the chair behind me. "I'm not ready to talk to you right now," I say, looking down at my food. Avery doesn't move. She stands there, crying quietly. Anywhere else I'd be worried about what people would think, seeing a crying girl in the middle of the cafeteria, but at this school, where traumatic memories pop up everywhere, everyone just kind of rolls with it.

"Lucy, please—"

I look up. And I shake my head. I see the anguish on Avery's face, like a million tiny lines etched on her skin, and it's more than I can handle. I don't know what to do with it. I go back to focusing on unwrapping my sandwich, and I don't look at her again for the rest of the period.

At the end of lunch, Avery slides me a piece of paper torn from her notebook.

Lucy,

I have never been so sorry. I messed up. I never should have told anyone your secret. Can we please be friends again? Please? And it's not just because you're my only friend.

    I miss you because I like you. I miss you because, in your own sarcastic way, you're funny. I miss you because you're nice. I miss you because you listen when I talk.

    Please give me a chance to make it up to you. Life is too short—I can't stand how I hurt you, so please let me try again.

                    Avery

She's gone from the cafeteria before I finish reading, but I know instantly that I am ready to forgive her.

And now that I know that, it's all I want to do. I don't want to forget what she did, or say it's okay, because it definitely wasn't, but I do want to try being friends again. I think of Theo, of the twenty-seven kids who died in Queensland. Like Avery wrote, life is way too short. I want to give her another chance.

∞

It's harder than I thought it would be to find Avery after school. There is no mime today. I can't remember what her last class is, and the hallway is a teeming mass of faces and hair and tote bags and people buried in their text conversations. Now that Avery's hair is blond, she blends in a lot more than she did as Cleopatra/Elizabeth Taylor when I first met her.

I'm about to give up and just take the bus home and call her—when I see her waiting by the front office. She's sitting on a bench outside the glass door, and I walk right over.

"Hey," I say. I have no idea how I will get home, since I will definitely miss my bus now, but I don't care.

"Oh, hi," she says, surprised to see me there. She stands up and blurts out, "I'm so sorry."

"Thanks," I say. "I read your note."

She just nods, waiting for me to continue.

"I really want to give you another chance, to be friends again, but first there's some stuff I have to say."

Avery bursts into tears. "Oh, I'm so glad," she sobs. "I felt awful. I messed up so bad and I wouldn't blame you if you never forgave me."

I have an impulse to hug her, right here in full view of all the other kids who are rushing by, witnessing the drama unfolding between two misfits.

So I do hug her, and she just cries more.

"I'm so, so sorry," she says into my shoulder. I can feel her tears on my hair, but I don't mind. It feels good to hug a friend. It feels pretty great to forgive.

"I know," I say. Like Mr. Jackson said, I jumped in, and now I'm figuring it out as I go. "Can we talk somewhere else?" I ask, aware of all the eyes on us.

Avery nods, pulling away and wiping at her eyes. I shift my tote bag back onto my shoulder. Avery picks hers up from where she'd dropped it on the ground.

"I have to get some papers signed in there," she says, pointing toward the principal's office. "But I can meet you outside in ten minutes."

"Okay," I say. "But then how will we get home?"

Avery wipes at her face some more. "My grandma is going to pick me up. She can drop you off too."

I grin. It feels great to have a friend again, and not just for the transportation options. We haven't fixed everything between us, but I feel certain now that the equation has a solution, even if we don't know the answer yet. We at least know what we're working on.

By the time Avery finds me out on the picnic tables along the side of the building, I've had more time to think of what I want to say to her. What I need to say.

"You really hurt me," I begin. "But I know you know that."

Avery nods.

The next part is harder. I take a deep breath. "I guess I just need to know why you told them about Theo. When I'd asked you not to tell anyone. I need to understand why you did that."

Avery takes a deep breath too. "Yeah," she says in a thoughtful voice. "I've been wondering the same thing. I was up all night thinking about it. It wasn't something I planned to do." She starts to cry again, and for a second I'm tempted to tell her to forget the whole thing because the crying is making me uncomfortable, but I know we need to finish this conversation.

"I guess I got scared," she says. I watch her intently. "That you were making other friends, like Joshua, and all the kids in mime. And then you wouldn't need me anymore. If you had other friends, they wouldn't want to associate with me, so you'd ditch me."

"But I wouldn't do that!" I say. "And by the way, I truly did not know about you and Joshua. I had no idea I would hurt you by holding hands with him. How was I supposed to know you liked him?"

Avery rolls her eyes. "Well, it's stupid, but when you told me you had a crush on him, and I said that he and I used to be close, well . . ." She trails off. "I guess that wasn't really clear at all. There was no way you could have known."

Avery looks up at the sky, her tears pooling in her blue eyes, shining in the sun.

"I got scared," she says again. "And I figured maybe I should just end our friendship before you had a chance to. I would push you away before you could leave me behind."

There's a long silence. My head swims in it. An unknown: *the value or quantity to be discovered by solving an equation.* I never realized there could be so many things I didn't know.

We both stare into the distance, where the soccer teams are setting up for practice. The kids on the field are wearing uniforms, bright blue and green against the dry grass.

We're silent for a long time. I think about how there's always so much going on inside people's heads that you can't even possibly guess. Like how I had no idea Avery liked Joshua, too, even though she thought it was implied. I wonder at all the other things people are thinking that I can't possibly imagine. All those unknowns in each person's head.

"I want to be someone you can trust," Avery says. "I promise I would never tell your secrets again."

"And I want you to know I would never ditch you, no matter how many other friends I have," I say, thinking of how Mr. Jackson said he thought all the kids in mime would be my friends if I wanted.

"I know you mean that," Avery says, still looking off at the soccer fields, "but people here just hate me."

I gasp. "No, I'm sure they don't hate you."

Avery rolls her eyes. "Okay, fine, maybe hate is simplistic. But they sure don't want to be around me."

"They don't know you."

"They think they do. They know what Damien did, and I get it. My therapist says sometimes people need space from things that retraumatize them."

Maybe, I think, but the kids here are more open about their traumas than anyone I've ever met. They face so much head-on. Why did they all have to pick this one thing—this one person—to avoid?

"I honestly don't blame them," Avery adds. "I don't even think they're trying to be mean. They don't make fun of me or play pranks on me or even really talk about me behind my back. They just pretend I don't exist."

I shake my head. "It's still not fair."

"You can say that again," Avery says, starting to smile a tiny bit.

So I do. "It's so not fair. Life isn't fair." I've been wanting to say this to Avery since the day that girl cut in front of her in the cafeteria line. To tell Avery she deserves better.

Of course, we both understand better than most people how unfair life can be. And I know I can't make any guarantees to Avery. But I also know I want to be her friend. So I sit with her, for as long as she wants, until she calls her grandmother to take us home.

∞

Before I get out of the car, Avery asks me to wait. Her grandmother is listening to NPR blare loudly from the ancient speakers, and I sit in the smoky-smelling back seat next to Avery while she flips through her sketchbook and finds a page, tearing it out neatly and carefully, like the note she wrote me at lunch.

"I wanted to give this to you," she says quietly. Her grandmother doesn't turn around; she's not paying any attention to us. "It's a poem I wrote."

"Wow, cool," I say. "Poetry."

She shrugs, clearly uncomfortable. "It's one of those things my therapist suggested a long time ago, and I kind of liked writing it, so it's become, you know, something I do."

She hands me the paper. "You won't show it to anyone?" she asks. Her eyes are still red from crying earlier.

"Of course not," I promise.

"Okay."

"Okay." I open the car door, the poem clutched in my hand. I can't wait to get inside and read it.

"Thanks for the ride," I call out to Avery's grandmother. She doesn't respond, and I don't know if she heard me, but I close the door anyway and walk to my house. When I get to the front door, I turn to wave at the dusty gray sedan, but it's already gone. The sun is setting and it's almost dark, the wispy clouds thin on the horizon. Bare trees make a stark outline against the sky.

As soon as I'm surrounded by the warm air of the front hall, I put down my bag and read Avery's poem.

Family, it's called.

Where there once were brothers
Empty rooms now stand
Where there once were sisters
No one to hold a hand

Where there once were parents
Different people sit
Some of them have disappeared
We don't understand a bit

And where there once was promise
A future we could see
Now there is confusion
Who knows what it will be?

But there's a sister out there
Who's lonely, just like me
Another kind of family
The one we choose to be

I'm crying before I've gotten to the end. Of course I'm sad for Avery—for everyone Damien hurt, including her. And of course, I ache for Theo and all the things that should have been.

But there's another feeling too. I'm not so alone anymore. Yes, Avery's loss of her brother was different in a lot of ways, and Damien was definitely completely different from Theo. Still, we each lost a brother—along with the lives we used to have. And you can't place a value on loss; one is not greater than the other. They both just plain hurt. Avery has granted us the same level of grief. $X = Y$.

I press the paper to my chest and let the words sink in, like a line intersecting my clothes, through my skin, into my heart.

CHAPTER 17

Which of the following does not equal 3/4?
a) -3/-4
b) 75/100
c) 9/16
d) all of the above

A shocking thing happens the week after my fight with Avery. At lunch on Thursday, Shontay joins us at our table. She sits next to me, far from Avery, but she's at our table.

"I think we should change the ending of our scene," she says to Avery, and before I can get over my surprise, the two of them pick up a discussion from mime class two days ago, about the scene they're developing together.

When Cory slides into a seat next to Shontay

a few minutes later, I wonder if Mr. Jackson told them to sit with us, as some kind of assignment for mime. But I realize that it's unlikely that he did— and honestly, I don't care why they're sitting with us. People are talking to Avery during school, people besides me, and it feels really, really good. I catch Avery's eye. We grin.

"Are you excited for the mime show?" I ask Avery later, as we walk to fifth period. It feels like the tide is turning and everything is going to be better.

Avery's face falls. "No," she says.

"Why not? I'm not that thrilled about performing in front of a crowd, but Mr. Jackson is so proud of us, and he's so enthusiastic about us showing off our work . . ." I trail off as I see how upset Avery is getting.

"My mom doesn't come to these kinds of things," she says in a strained voice. "She doesn't like to be in public. She thinks people only see Damien when they see her, even though they weren't even technically related."

Kids rush past us in the hallway, opening and closing lockers.

I frown. "That sucks." I reach out and squeeze her arm, because I don't know how else to tell her that I care. That I'm sorry that everything can't be fixed by a few new friends at our lunch table.

Avery nods and tries to smile. "Thanks."

∞

We have one more mime class before our performance. Everyone is getting a little bit nervous, but Rosemary reassures all of us.

"My aunt, who is a professional actor, says a little bit of nerves before a show is normal, and even helpful. You'll forget about being nervous as soon as the curtain goes up." We've been hearing even more than usual about this aunt over the past few weeks, but no one so much as rolls their eyes at Rosemary. Maybe, like me, they love these little tidbits.

We've all arranged to stay an hour later than usual, working out the shape of the show as a whole, with each scene a vital part. Shontay and Peter have ended up making a comedy routine out of their how-to-open-a-door dispute, and Joshua has teamed up with Marcus and Henry for a sketch about baseball. I'm not sure I totally get it, but the three of them think it's hilarious, and Mr. Jackson says it has good prop work—holding an invisible bat and catching an invisible ball. And I love watching Joshua perform it, because his hands don't clench and unclench at all while he's onstage. He seems really happy and comfortable. I try not to be obvious, but I could watch him all day.

Rosemary and Sarita are going to do a scene about babies. They rock the imaginary babies and push them in imaginary strollers. Whenever I watch them in rehearsal, I think of Theo and the time my mom mimed holding him. I wonder if my parents will think of that too when they're watching the show. I hope it doesn't make them too sad.

There are a few big group scenes—one where we all get to freestyle dance like we did on the first day of class, and of course the final scene that's all about loss. Luckily that one is pretty vague and abstract, and I hope that my parents won't know I'm thinking of Theo the whole way through. Or maybe it would be good if they did know.

As it turns out, I'm the only one who is going to be doing a solo piece. It's toward the end, but I'm not at all nervous. I've practiced and practiced, with Mr. Jackson and Avery giving notes. When I'm rehearsing on the cafetorium stage, with the lights on me, I feel oddly alone but in a happy way, and I get lost in my story. I fire up my spaceship, and I watch the world around me change. I find myself smiling a lot, even where it wasn't in the script.

"This is one fantastic show you all have created," Mr. Jackson tells us after class. "It's going to be wonderful. You've got this."

I look around at the faces I've come to know so well. My classmates—my friends, maybe. And I feel a rush of gratitude that mime doesn't use words. I'm not sure I will ever know how to talk to these people about big, important stuff, like the shooting they all lived through. But now at least I know how to just be with them. I know how to observe, and how to accept what they choose to share in the ways they choose to share it, and how to be part of the team.

I'm not quite one of them. But we are all points on a graph together. Where I once thought that there could be no connection between us, since we don't make a straight line, I see now that maybe we form something else. We are a function, sine or cosine, waves that rise and fall, including each point across one plane. We are like waves, full of highs and lows. Not everything in life has to be a straight line. If you're willing to bend a little bit, you can be part of a whole ocean.

CHAPTER 18

Question: How many times can you subtract 5 from 25?

Answer: Only once, because then you're subtracting 5 from 20.

"But aren't mimes supposed to have painted faces?" Cory asks.

Shontay rolls her eyes. "You're thinking of clowns." She pulls her hair into a ponytail, looking in the mirror of the makeshift dressing room Mr. Jackson has set up for us in the teachers' lounge. It's located conveniently behind the stage, and it still smells faintly of cigarette smoke from thirty years ago when teachers were allowed to smoke in here.

Mr. Jackson brought in some mirrors, and there's a pitcher of water and a stack of plastic cups on a table. Everyone has tossed bags and coats on the couch, so there's nowhere to sit. Avery and I are putting on our long-sleeved black T-shirts over the tank tops we decided we'd wear under them.

"In case the lights make the T-shirts see-through," Avery said yesterday. She doesn't want anyone to see that she doesn't wear a bra, and I don't want anyone to see that I do.

Rosemary bursts in carrying an armload of flowers. "My aunt, the actress, said everyone should get flowers on opening night." She begins to hand out the individually wrapped stems—a mix of red roses and white carnations.

Joshua is the only boy who says thank you to her, and it makes me like him even more. We've still never acknowledged the hand-holding thing. And maybe that's for the best. It's not like I'm going to go up to him and say, "Hey, remember when the fire alarm went off and you cried? And I held your hand? Wasn't that great?"

But occasionally, our eyes will meet across a room, or he'll make me laugh with a well-timed pratfall during math class—a nod to our mime connection—and my heart does these little acrobatic tricks.

Mr. Jackson knocks on the door. "Everyone decent in there?" he asks before entering.

Avery laughs. "It's not like anyone was going to strip down in here in front of each other!" she says quietly to me. The rule is that any actual changing of clothes has to happen in the bathrooms.

Mr. Jackson tells us we have ten more minutes until the show is going to start. "Last calls for bathrooms and water drinking and anything else you have to attend to before curtain," he says, sounding very professional.

When he gathers us in a circle five minutes later, Mr. Jackson dims the lights. We all take deep breaths together, as he instructs. There is so much electric energy in the room that it's almost buzzing with it.

"Whatever happens out there onstage tonight," Mr. Jackson says quietly, looking from face to face as he speaks, "I've never been more proud of a group of students." His eyes meet mine last, and he smiles. I press my lips together to keep my emotions from spilling over.

"You've all worked so hard. Not just on your scenes, which are fabulous, but on the process of becoming a team. A community. And that is more important to me than any performance."

Every face in the room is beaming.

"Now go out there and have fun," Mr. Jackson says.

We take our places on the stage, where the curtains are closed to keep the audience from seeing us yet. From her place next to me, Avery leans over and gives me a hug.

"Break a leg," she whispers.

"You too."

∞

Mr. Jackson told us it didn't matter what happened out on the stage, but the show goes basically perfectly. It's just as we rehearsed. Maybe a little faster, because of all our nervous energy, but there are no big mistakes or disasters. By the time we take our final bow together, it's all a blur in my mind. Like points that make up a line, I can't remember the individual moments, I just know that the thing as a whole—the line, or the show in this case—is complete, and it feels amazing.

Afterward, we go out into the seating area to find the people who came to see us. My parents hug me, both at the same time. My dad has tears in his eyes.

"I loved watching you on the stage," he says, patting my back.

My mom holds me for a long, long time. "We're so proud of you."

I look around. Joshua's parents must have gotten a babysitter for his sister, because I see two adults embracing him as well. Shontay's dad is taking tons of pictures. Rosemary's moms are both there, and her older sister too. Several of the other performers are talking to friends who showed up to support them. I didn't even know other students would be coming tonight. Avery stands alone, scanning the crowd.

It's like watching another mime performance. No words, and Avery's face tells the whole story. Her mom is clearly not there. I wonder where her grandparents are, until I remember that Avery said they don't like to drive at night. I feel so sad I think I might cry.

"Isn't that your friend?" my mom asks, seeing me looking at Avery. I nod.

"Let's go over there," my dad says. "I have to ask her what in the world she likes about *Citizen Kane*."

I grin, glad he remembers that she's the one who recommended it. And suddenly, we're surrounding

Avery. My mom hugs her. My dad talks to her about movies. Mr. Jackson comes over too, and when Mr. Jackson hugs Avery and tells her that her piece with Shontay and Cory was perfect, she really looks happy. I know it doesn't make up for her mom not being there, but it helps.

"Great job," says a voice behind me. When I turn, I'm shocked to see the kids from my bus stop—Dave and the blond boy, whom I now know is named Ethan—in a group with a few other people I recognize from school. I look behind me, assuming they're talking to someone else, but I'm in front of a wall. There's no one else they could be speaking to.

"Um, thanks," I say nervously. I realize I haven't had a conversation with either of them since they told me about Avery's brother months ago. I've avoided them, and they've seemed to be happy to ignore me. Until now, apparently.

Ethan smiles. "I really liked the thing you did about the rocket ship." I blink in surprise.

"You know who would have liked this class?" Dave says. "Bette. She would have wanted to be onstage in something like this. In elementary school whenever there was a talent show or our music class did a performance, she always got really into it."

I don't know what to say in reply, but I feel a smile on my face. Of all the times I've thought of Bette, all the nights I've slept in her—our—room, all the questions I've had about her, all the times I imagined her as a friend . . . I never *really* knew anything about her likes or dislikes. Who she actually was. I gathered the numerical information, like her birth date and death date, her age—the statistics. But Bette isn't numbers. She was a person. And in a small way, it's like Dave has brought her into this moment to share it with us.

"Thank you," I say to Dave, making eye contact with him for the first time ever. And even though it probably doesn't really make sense for me to thank him, Dave smiles. I think he understands why I said that.

∞

After the show, the whole mime class is going to Friendly's together. The parents miraculously agree to drop us all off and come back in an hour. They must be really proud, because my parents usually aren't on board with that kind of stuff.

This Friendly's looks exactly like the one we used

to go to in Maryland. My mom, my dad, and Theo and I went there for ice cream a few times.

The ten of us crowd noisily around the hostess station, waiting to be seated. Everyone is talking and laughing.

"I think he likes you," Avery says to me quietly. I follow her eyes to where Joshua stands.

I blush instinctively. "No," I say.

"Yes," Avery says, all seriousness. "And I don't ever want it to be weird between us, because of him or any other guy or any other friend."

I watch Joshua, clenching and unclenching his hands as he glances over at me. He smiles. I smile back.

"Are you sure?" I ask Avery.

She nods solemnly. "Go over there and hold his hand for real," she says, giving me a nudge.

I look at my friend. "Avery. It's not a big deal. You're more important."

Avery takes my left hand in her right and gives it a squeeze. "I mean it. I want you to be happy. Go flirt with Joshua."

I giggle. Out of the corner of my eye, I can see Joshua steal another glance over at me. He's talking to Marcus and Henry, laughing along with them.

"Besides," Avery continues, "we're in seventh grade. It's not like you're getting married or anything."

"Ew!" I say. "Definitely not."

Avery looks at me again. "I mean it. Go for it. I will not be jealous or do anything stupid."

"Promise?"

"Promise." She grins. "Well, I might tease you a little, in private of course . . ."

I swat her playfully on the arm. "Whatever."

Joshua is full-on looking at me now. The hostess comes to show us to our table, and as we follow her in a herd, I find myself between Avery and Joshua. Sitting between the two of them is the closest thing to pure happiness that I have felt in a long, long time.

Cory, who's sitting on Avery's other side, says something to Avery that I don't quite catch. Avery answers them, sounding casual, but I know it's a huge deal for Cory to still be talking to her now that the show is over.

"You were great in the show," Joshua says quietly to me. I can feel him breathing, he's so close. His shirt is touching my arm, the soft blue cotton tickling my bare skin.

"Thanks. So were you."

And, underneath the table, where no one else can see, Joshua takes my hand in his.

"Is this okay?" he asks, just as I did during the fire drill, which feels like years ago instead of weeks.

I nod and, ever so gently, I squeeze his hand. He squeezes back. There is nothing scared or sad about it. He is holding my hand because he wants to.

∞

This time, the family meeting is my father's idea. I find the note in the morning before school.

Why was the math book so sad?
(Answer: Because it had too many problems.)
But I don't want that poor book to be sad all the time. So . . . let's cheer it up? Family meeting. Living room. Tonight.
Love,
The Mysterious Math Joker.
Just kidding.
Love,
Dad

Dad has decided to take up cooking, so tonight he makes dinner and asks me to be his helper. It turns out I'm really good at it. I love how recipes are so mathematical. There are steps and measurements, and everything is precise.

While we're in the kitchen, figuring things out as we go along, I can almost imagine that Theo is still alive, as if maybe he's in another room playing or sleeping. These kinds of daydreams used to make me sad, but tonight, as Dad and I crouch in front of the oven trying to see if the food is cooking properly, they make me smile.

The food turns out okay, and after we've eaten, the three of us sit down, just like we did weeks ago when I taught them charades. I can tell my dad is uncomfortable. He looks around, anywhere but at our eyes, and shifts his weight next to my mom on the gray love seat.

"Lucy," he says finally, "for a long time, I've been a little dismissive of your mom's . . . coping strategies. The fundraising stuff isn't for me anymore, but it's great for your mom, and it's meaningful work, and I respect that. I also really admire that your mom goes to therapy. That she's working on . . . everything. And I've decided I'm going to start too."

I look at my mom, who is grinning. She takes his hand. They've obviously talked about this ahead of telling me, and my mom seems thrilled.

"That's great, Dad." I feel lighter, like a balloon being given a burst of helium.

"And we think you should talk to someone too," he says. I look back and forth between my parents, confused. Do they think I'm not doing so well? I feel better these days than I have in a long time.

"It's not a punishment," my mother says quickly. "And it's not because we don't want you to share things with *us*. We really want to work on being able to voice our difficult feelings and to listen when you voice yours. You can be open and honest with us, but you also deserve to do that with a professional who knows how to help you process it all."

"Is that something you'd like?" my dad asks.

I consider it for a moment and nod. "Yeah," I say. "I think I would."

"We can go all together, or you can go on your own," says my mom.

"Or both," Dad adds.

I stand up to hug them, but my parents rush to me first, before I can take a step to shorten the line of distance between us as individual points. They wrap me up again, and we're one shape. We're a polyhedron: solid, three-dimensional. A family.

When we separate, my mom gestures for us to sit down, though this time, she's next to me on the love seat and my dad moves the chair closer to us.

"And to get us in the right frame of mind for therapy," she says, "We thought we'd try something today."

My dad seems uncomfortable again. Nervous, even. He looks at the floor. I remember that we're here because I asked him to talk about Theo more, and I know how hard this is for him.

"Lucy, do you want to share some memories of Theo?" he says after a while.

I look at Mom. "Where do I start?"

Mom smiles. "What do you remember?" She shrugs, as if anything and everything would be okay to say.

"He used to make me laugh."

Mom grins now, her face lighting up in a way we don't see much. "Yes. He was funny. He had a good sense of humor."

"Remember when he was, like, one or maybe a little older," I say, "and he figured out that if he dropped toys from his high chair, one of us would come over and pick them up?"

Mom and I laugh. Dad is still, like a statue. "And at first we thought he was just really clumsy," Mom adds.

"Yeah," I say, picturing little Theo with a devilish grin on his face, "and then we realized he just thought it was fun to watch us scurry around frantically every time he dropped something."

"He would do it on purpose—remember, Beau?" Mom turns to look at Dad.

I'm scared to look, afraid of what I will find on my father's face. Tears? Nothing at all?

But I do look, and I'm instantly glad I did. My father is smiling. A real, genuine smile.

"And he loved that ridiculous song, remember?" my dad says. He starts humming the tune.

Mom whistles and taps out the rhythm of the song's opening. I remember it too—a goofy, very 1970s song with the kind of infectious melody that can get stuck in your head for days.

Dad says, "I think he made me play that song on repeat for six hours straight one time."

Mom laughs. "That sounds like Theo."

"It didn't stop until my phone ran out of battery."

I keep waiting for their laughter to shatter, for the inevitable moment when it becomes tears. But this time, it doesn't. We sing some more. We laugh some more. And I think of infinity.

My parents' circles have merged, and together, they intersect. It's not just a figure eight. They make a perfect infinity sign, and Theo and I are part of it too, because we are part of them. We are linked forever, and we go on and on and on. Like Theo, listening to the song on repeat. Like our laughter this evening. Like the waves of the ocean Theo pointed at. Like love. Like infinity.

EPILOGUE

The week after our mime performance, there's a math quiz. There's no extra credit question on this one, but when I finish all the problems with time to spare, I look at the blank space on the bottom of the second page.

I know that, a few seats away, Joshua is clenching and unclenching his hands as he does the problem sets. I know that a few rooms down the hall, Avery is doing a presentation in history. I know that, in the city, my parents are working hard, and I know that, somewhere, somehow, Theo's memory is floating on the wind or in the sky, whispering to me just when I think I'm out of hope.

I look at the blank, white space on the paper and start to write.

Extra Credit? ☺

I thought of something else that is infinite. Grief. Grief is infinite. You may think you're over it, but there's always another step to take before you actually get to the wall. And that means you're never really there.

But the good news is that love is infinite too. And friendship can be infinite. There's always more between you and wherever the wall is. And more and more and more.

I stop to reread what I've written. I know it's a little messy and my thoughts are all over the place, but I also know that Mr. Jackson will understand. I hope that when he reads it, he knows I'm trying to say thank you.

AUTHOR'S NOTE

The idea for this book came to me after the mass shooting in San Bernardino, California, in 2015. I had a tiny baby and a four year old, and I didn't know how to process my feelings of helplessness and my fears about the world in which they are growing up. I wanted to be an advocate for change, but I wasn't sure exactly how I'd use my voice.

For me, writing *AfterMath* was a step in a longer journey. Some of the seeds of it came from my grandfather, Alan Barth, whom I never met, but who influenced me greatly. He was an avid believer in the First Amendment, in equal rights for all, and in commonsense gun control laws. I may not have known him, but thanks to his powerful writing, I grew up knowing what mattered to him, and that became part of me.

I wrote the original draft of this book long before the shooting at Marjorie Stoneman Douglas High School in Parkland, Florida, but the voices of the brave survivors who got the nation's attention motivated me to stick with this story, as did the memories of the lives lost there and in every gun-related tragedy. There are too many to mention here, and they are each devastating and important to remember. My primary goal in writing *AfterMath* has been to be respectful of them and their loved ones. I hope I've succeeded.

I have, of course, drawn on my own personal experiences of grief and trauma for certain aspects of the story. I have been the kid who couldn't stop talking about something that happened to me, shocking plenty of adults who expected me to process my pain differently. This novel was also influenced by the experiences of my friend Mary Ann Rogers-Witte Ciciarelli and her precious son, Lee. Thank you for sharing your story and for showing that even the briefest lives have a never-ending impact.

I couldn't have written this book without guidance from the many mental health professionals I spoke to. I hope that readers come away from the book with a sense that therapy is always a good idea, and that talking to someone really helps. Let's end the stigma around mental health. Everyone is working through something; no one should have to do that alone.

ACKNOWLEDGMENTS

I'm full of gratitude to everyone who has had anything to do with this book or with me over the past six years. Especially Hanna Neier, my one-person village; Jordan Scott, equal parts my first copy editor and my best cheerleader; Mike Stickle, the person who told me I was a writer; Nora Zelevansky and Katie Schorr, who (along with Hanna Neier) are the best writers group a person could ever have. I TRULY could not have done this without you.

Thanks to all the friends who've supported me along this journey, including Diane Tosh, Tamar Huberman, Ryan Cunningham, Caryn Gorden, and the Cricket Buddies, Rebecca Gifford Goldberg and Jenny Lang. To Toby Orenstein and Carole Graham Lehan for teaching me to be a storyteller. To Rachel Hamilton, mentor extraordinaire, friend, and example. To Katy Tosh, Sarah Tosh, Anna Norman, Bethany McCall, and every babysitter who made it possible to write this book. I absolutely wouldn't be writing these words now were it not for the pizza bites and peanut butter sandwiches you made, picture books you read, playground trips you took, and snuggles you gave to my little loves while Jim and I worked. You are the heroes.

Kari Sutherland, agent extraordinaire, you are patient and kind, encouraging and thoughtful—everything I needed. Thanks for never giving up on me or on this book. I can never thank you enough. Amy Fitzgerald, you are the editor of my dreams. Every single thing you suggest or fix is gold, and I'm a better writer for having worked with you. Thank you for believing in this book, for "getting" it, for loving it for what it is. And a big thanks to the whole team at Lerner/Carolrhoda, including creative director Danielle Carnito, production designer Erica Johnson, and cover illustrator Dien Ton That.

So many thanks to the extraordinary women in the literary world who have offered me support, guidance, and wisdom over the years: Emilia Rhodes (my very first editor, always!), Tina DuBois, Sara Crowe, Sara Shandler, Melissa Walker, Alex

Richards, Holly Root, Nicola Kraus, Una LaMarche, Yona McDonough, Toby Devens, Amelia Kahaney, Helen Phillips, and especially Amanda Maciel.

To the women (and men) of The Pile: Everything I want to say to you all is private and profane. But know that I love you all so so so so so much. I finally want to be part of a club that will have me as a member! Imagine that.

And to my family:

Barbara Dobkin, your enthusiasm for and belief in me and in this book are an immeasurable gift. You opened the world for me. You made me want to be an activist. I owe so much to you. But mostly, I just freaking love you.

Omry and Amy Preiser Maoz (and Nate and Ben), my family away from family, I love you all so much. Thank you for being our modern and secular kibbutz.

Jim Isler, you are everything. Thanks for seeing me through all the stages that got us to the current butterfly that I am (and that this book is). I love you. Here's to the future!

Hallie and Max Isler, you two have taught me so much. You are true gifts, and I love you both more than you'll ever know.

Ellen Barth, my original teammate, you are the best thing ever.

My parents, Andy and Toba Barth, for a million things—but mostly just for loving me. That's all that really matters.

Robert and Susan Isler, Nancy and Michael Strong, Eric Dobkin, Rachel Dobkin, Flora Wolf, Abigail and Susannah Wolf, Frank and Nada Isler, Brian Elieson, Tom Isler, Lavanya Kondapalli, Leo, Felix, and Jayani—I love you all very much.

I've never been much of a fangirl, but I have to mention Mike Schur, who has long inspired me to make art that really means something to people. You have no idea of the gifts you've given us.

To Eric Ebersole and Terry Sullivan, who inspired and shaped Mr. Jackson's character in this book, I'm forever grateful. Mr. Ebersole, your teaching of Zeno's paradox stuck with me, obviously, but you taught me so much more than that. Mr. Sullivan, you were the first teacher who saw the writer in me. Thanks for teaching us mime that one year. I really needed it.

In researching and thinking about the topic of gun violence, I've found numerous resources to be helpful, including those provided by Sandy Hook

Promise, a nonprofit dedicated to preventing gun violence through education and advocacy. As a member of Moms Demand Action for Gun Sense in America and its umbrella organization, Everytown for Gun Safety, I'm grateful to all those who work toward gun violence prevention.

Finally, to all the beautiful souls killed in senseless gun violence and to their loved ones who are left behind: We see you. We will always remember you. We will never stop fighting to honor you by making the world a safer and kinder place.

QUESTIONS FOR DISCUSSION

1. Why did Lucy's parents move to Queensland? Do you think their reasoning makes sense? Why or why not?

2. According to Lucy, how is her grief for Theo different from what her new classmates have gone through?

3. Why do you think so many kids immediately tell Lucy about their experiences of the shooting? Why does this shock Lucy?

4. Why is Lucy so curious about Bette, the girl who used to live in her house? What does she eventually learn about what Bette was actually like?

5. Why does Lucy like the math jokes that her dad leaves for her? What does this ritual show you about Lucy's relationship with her dad?

6. What does Lucy like about mime? How does it help her?

7. What are the limits of mime? What can it *not* do for Lucy?

8. Why do the other kids avoid Avery? How does this affect her?

9. Make a list of things that help Lucy express and deal with her feelings throughout the story. What activities help you work through difficult feelings?

10. Throughout the book, Lucy struggles to understand the concept of infinity. Name some examples of infinity that show up in the story.

ABOUT THE AUTHOR

Emily Barth Isler lives in Los Angeles with her husband and their two kids. *AfterMath* is her first novel. Find her at www.emilybarthisler.com.